Disney Princess

ALSO FROM JOE BOOKS

Disney Princess Comics Treasury
Disney Frozen Cinestory Comic
Disney Cinderella Cinestory Comic
Disney Alice in Wonderland Cinestory Comic
Disney Princess Comic Strips Collection Volume One
Disney Princess Comic Strips Collection Volume Two
Disney Tangled Cinestory Comic
Disney Tangled Before Ever After Cinestory Comic
Disney Beauty and the Beast Cinestory Comic
Disney Tangled: The Story of the Movie in Comics
Disney Snow White and the Seven Dwarfs: The Story of the Movie in Comics
Disney The Little Mermaid: The Story of the Movie in Comics
Disney Beauty and the Beast: As Told by Emoji Cinestory Comic
Disney Snow White and the Seven Dwarfs Cinestory Comic
Disney Snow White and the Seven Dwarfs Cinestory Comic Collector's Edition
Disney Princess Comic Strips Collection: Something to Sing About

Disney Princess

The Enchanted Collection

JOE BOOKS LTD

Published simultaneously in the United States and Canada by Joe Books Ltd,
489 College Street, Suite 203, Toronto, ON M6G 1A5.

www.joebooks.com

First Joe Books edition: March 2018

Print ISBN: 978-1-77275-750-7

Library and Archives Canada Cataloguing in Publication information is available upon request.

Printed and bound in Canada
1 3 5 7 9 10 8 6 4 2

TABLE OF CONTENTS

Snow White

RISE AND SHINE

BASHFUL

NOW YOU RELAX AND TELL ME WHAT IS WRONG.

DO YOU NEED SOME SPACE?

IS THIS BETTER? FARTHER?

I SAID, *"IS THIS FAR ENOUGH?"*

I'M SORRY, BUT YOU'LL HAVE TO SPEAK UP. IT'S HARD TO HEAR YOU OVER THE RAIN.

THUMP

THUMP
AND THUNDER!

OH, BASHFUL! THAT GUITAR IS OFF KEY.
BAD KEY? IS THAT IT? YOU NEED A KEY?

IT'S A GOOD THING I KEEP A SPARE.
NOTHING LIKE WAITING IN THE RAIN AFTER A HARD DAY'S WORK.
End

FANCY DANCING

ARE YOU SURE YOU'RE AWAKE ENOUGH TO DANCE, SLEEPY?
READY AND ABLE.

MAYBE YOU SHOULD TAKE A LITTLE NAP.
I'LL BE... FINE.

I'VE GOT AN IDEA. WAIT RIGHT THERE.

OH DEAR! I DON'T THINK WE CAN BRING YOUR BED TO THE ROYAL BALL.
...THEN WE SHOULD...USE A BED...FROM THE PALACE... ZZZ...
SLEEPY

I DO LOVE HOW YOU'RE ALWAYS SO HAPPY, HAPPY.
I LOVE IT, TOO, MA'AM! HA HA HA!

BUT A ROYAL BALL IS VERY SOPHISTICATED. WILL YOU BE ABLE TO ACT SOPHISTICATED?
WHY, I AIN'T EVEN ABLE TO PRONOUNCE...THAT WORD. HA HA HA!
BUT I'LL TRY, MA'AM. HERE I GO.

I THINK HE'S GONNA EXPLODE!
OH MY.
SOPHISTIMACATED HOGWASH!

BASHFUL, WOULD YOU LIKE TO DANCE WITH ME?
OHHHHHHHHHH GOSH! I WOULD LOVE TO.

WONDERFUL!
NOW, WOULD YOU LIKE TO STOP HIDING UNDERNEATH THAT BENCH?
OHHHHHHHHHH GOSH! I DON'T THINK SO.

OW! DOPEY, WATCH YOUR--OW!

PAY ATTENTION TO--OW!

OWWW! OH, THAT HURTS!
DOPEY, SHE TOLD US NOT TO STEP ON HER FEET! DON'T STEP ON HER FEET!

THAT'S OKAY, DOPEY. WE CAN KEEP DANCING, I'LL JUST CHANGE INTO THESE WOODEN SHOES.

WHEN'RE YA GONNA FACE FACTS? YOU'LL NEVER LEARN US HOW TO DANCE AT A ROYAL BALL.
OH, GRUMPY. DON'T SAY THAT.

ALL WE KNOWS IS THAT SILLY DANCIN', AND THAT AIN'T FIT FOR RACCOONS, LET ALONE ROYALTY.

I MEAN, ONLY A KING 'ER QUEEN COULD MAKE SILLY DANCIN' OKAY AT A ROYAL BALL!
WHY, OF COURSE. I'M A QUEEN!

GRUMPY, I COULD KISS YOU!
NOT IF YA CAN'T CATCH ME!

HO-LA-LA-EE-AY-EE-LA-EE-AY-EE-LEE-AY
THE QUEEN HAS VERY...INTERESTING FRIENDS.
YES. AREN'T THEY TERRIFIC?
End

BIRD SONGS

aaaaaahhh

aaaaahh——ah!

SKWANK

LIGHTER! TRY BREATHING FROM LOWER DOWN.

SNIFFFFF

SKWANK?

THAT'S GOING TO BE TOUGH TO HARMONIZE WITH.
fnrt!

THAT'S IT! I THINK WE'VE GOT IT!

Who?

A ***BARITONE!*** HOW SPLENDID!

YOU KEEP RHYTHM ON TWO AND FOUR, AND YOU HOLD THE LONG HIGH NOTES.

IF YOU CAN HANDLE BASS, I THINK THIS LITTLE FELLOW WILL BE A GREAT TREBLE.

AND YOU...

KEEP UP THE GOOD WORK. REMEMBER, LESS IS MORE!

ALL RIGHT, DO YOU ALL KNOW YOUR PARTS?

CRINKLE
SCHAFF
KKT

SKT KRICK SCUFFLE
WHAT IS THAT NOISE?

I'M SORRY. I SAID WE NEEDED A ***REST*** THERE!

HELLO! I DIDN'T SEE YOU THERE! DID YOU ENJOY THE CONCERT?

THE PLATYPUS WAS OFF-KEY.
End

BUDDY SYSTEM

I THINK THE TORTOISE MAKES AN **EXCELLENT** MATCH FOR YOU, BASHFUL.

WHAT DO YOU THINK?
OH... I DON'T KNOW...

COME, BASHFUL, AT LEAST TAKE A LOOK.
SHLOOP!

OOOH, HE'S A **HANDSOME** ONE!
HE'S INSIDE HIS SHELL, SILLY GOOSE.

I KNOW WHO WOULD MAKE A **PERFECT** FRIEND FOR YOU, SLEEPY.

BEARS HIBERNATE FOR MONTHS AT A TIME.
YAWN WHY?
Z

THEY'D RATHER STAY SNUGGLED UP THAN GO HUNTING FOR FOOD.

NO WONDER SLEEPY NEVER GETS UP FOR A MIDNIGHT SNACK.
ZZZ

HOW ABOUT A NICE CHIPMUNK FOR SNEEZY?
AHHHHH...

...CHOOO!
!

...CHOOO!
!!

NO FUR OR FEATHERS--I BELIEVE WE HAVE A **PERFECT** MATCH!

End

OFF TO WORK

WELL THEN, TODAY I'M GOING TO COME SEE THE MINE.

ALL IN FAVOR?
AYE!

AS USUAL, SLEEPY ABSTAINS.

HEIGH, HO. HEIGH, HO. IT'S OFF TO WORK WE GO!

WHAT FUN! DO YOU ALWAYS SING LIKE THIS ON YOUR WAY TO WORK?

WE SURE DO!

BUT WE USUALLY DON'T HAVE AN ARMY OF BEASTS TRAMPING ALONG BEHIND.

MY, IT CERTAINLY IS DARK IN THERE.

IT WAS DOPEY'S TURN TO BRING THE LANTERN.

AAH-AAAHH-AAAAAHHH.

THANKS FOR WAKING UP EARLY TO HELP US OUT, FRIENDS.
JUST THINK HOW MUCH WE COULD BE SAVING ON LANTERN FUEL EVERY YEAR!

GOLLY, THIS FIREFLY LIGHT SURE IS PRETTY!

AAAHHHHH...

...CHOOO!

MAYBE ONE OF US COULD RUN HOME TO GET A LANTERN?

THESE ARE HEAVY. IT TOOK ME YEARS TO GET STRONG ENOUGH TO USE ONE.

THEY ARE AWFULLY HEAVY.

"I GUESS CLEANING UP GETS ME MORE EXERCISE THAN I THOUGHT."

MINING IS THIRSTY WORK, BUT IT MUST ALL BE WORTH IT WHEN YOU FIND A JEWEL.

PFFT JEWELS ARE FINE, I GUESS.

I JUST LIKE HAVING SOMETHING I'M ALLOWED TO TAKE OUT MY FRUSTRATIONS ON.

OH!

LOOK! I ALREADY FOUND A DIAMOND!

GREAT. TOSS IT OVER THERE WITH THE OTHERS.

THAT'S A PRETTY ONE!
THANK YOU, HAPPY.

BUT IN THE TIME IT TOOK ME TO FIND JUST ONE DIAMOND, YOU EACH MINED DOZENS.

IT TOOK ME MONTHS TO FIND ONE THIS PRETTY WHEN I FIRST STARTED, AND YOU DID IT ON YOUR FIRST DAY.

I GUESS YOU COULD CALL IT A "MINER" MIRACLE?

GREAT WORK TODAY, SNOW!

NOW I KNOW WHY YOU ALL COME HOME SO DIRTY.

THANKS FOR BRUSHING THE DUST AWAY, FRIENDS!

UGH! AS IF TAKING A REGULAR BATH WEREN'T BAD ENOUGH!

End

HELPFUL HELPERS

SNORING

ZZZZZZZ! SNORT ZZZZZ!
I HEAR WHAT YOU MEAN.
SLEEPY

IT SOUNDS LIKE HE CAUGHT SNEEZY'S COLD.

MAYBE WE CAN OFFER HIM A HANDKERCHIEF TO BLOW HIS NOSE.
SLEEPY

SNNNNKKK!
SLEEPY

SLEEPY? WAKE UP! YOU'RE SNORING.

WHAT? HUH? OH, SORRY.

SEE? ISN'T THAT BETTER?

ZZZZZZZ!

PERHAPS SOME FRESH AIR WILL DO US ALL SOME GOOD.

IT'S SO PEACEFUL OUT HERE.
YOU CAN TAKE A BREATH, RELAX, AND--
ZZZZZ!!!

I DON'T THINK THIS IS A VERY GOOD IDEA.
IT'S A GREAT IDEA! NOBODY CAN HEAR ME DOWN HERE, SO GRUMPY CAN GET SOME SLEEP HIMSELF!
BE CAREFUL!
COME GET ME WHEN YOU WAKE UP!

THAT REALLY WAS KIND OF SLEEPY TO DO THIS FOR YOU.
HE NEEDED HIS SLEEP. I NEEDED A *MINE!*

NOW FOR SOME PEACE AND QUIET!
SLEEPY'S SNORES WON'T BOTHER YOU ONE BIT TONIGHT.

SLEEP TIGHT! I WON'T TELL ANYONE YOU WERE SMILING!

ZZZZZZZZZ

EARTHQUAKE!!!
End

BUCKETHEAD

OH, PRINCE BUCKETHEAD? I HAVE A SURPRISE!

I HAVE A NEW HAT! IT MATCHES MY GOWN!

WELL, THERE'S NO NEED FOR *IMPERTINENCE*, SIR!
End

BEDTIME STORY

THERE YOU GO! IS EVERYONE TUCKED IN?

GOOD! NOW FOR YOUR BEDTIME STORY.
DOC
HAPP

ONCE UPON A TIME...

WHAT TIME? DAY OR NIGHT?
WAS IT SPRINGTIME? I LIKE SPRINGTIME!
WHY ONLY ONCE?
SAYS WHO?
WHEN EXACTLY?
WHO WAS THERE?

LET ME START OVER. ONCE UPON A SUMMER NIGHT'S TIME...
DOPEY
DOC

PROBABLY TOO HOT FOR ANY GOOD TO COME OF IT!
GRUMPY

OH, THAT'S WHERE THE STORY BEGINS!
SNEEZY

THAT'S ***WHEN*** IT BEGINS, TECHNICALLY.

ONCE UPON A SUMMER NIGHT, SOME "NO GOOD" THINGS WERE ABOUT TO HAPPEN!

TO WHO?

TO ***WHOM?***

I DON'T KNOW! SHE'S TELLING THE STORY!

THERE WAS A HANDSOME PRINCE IN A FAR-OFF LAND.

IF HE'S SO FAR OFF, WHY DIDN'T WE START THE STORY THERE?
SNE

BECAUSE THE FAIR MAIDEN IS RIGHT ***HERE!***

YEP! THERE SHE IS! AND SHE'S PRETTY!

DOES SHE GET TO MEET THIS HANDSOME PRINCE?

DOES SHE GO TO HIM? OR DOES HE FIND HER?
THEY PROBABLY DON'T HAVE ANYTHING IN COMMON.

WHO SAYS HI FIRST?
WHO PROPOSES TO WHOM?

HURRY UP! SOME OF US NEED TO GET TO SLEEP!

SHHH! NOW IF YOU'LL ALL GIVE ME THE CHANCE, WITHOUT INTERRUPTING, I'LL TELL YOU!

ONCE UPON A SUMMER NIGHT, BOTH HERE AND IN A FAR-OFF LAND...

THERE WAS A HANDSOME PRINCE AND A BEAUTIFUL MAIDEN!
SLEEPY

AND THEY MET AND LIVED HAPPILY EVER AFTER! THE END...AND GOOD NIGHT!
Z Z Z Z Z Z Z Z Z
THE MIDDLE ACT NEEDS WORK.
End

Cinderella

WHATEVER YOU WISH FOR

BIBBIDI BOBBIDI FLU

YOU TWO GET THE INGREDIENTS.
ZUK-ZUK!
YEAH, ZUK-ZUK!

SALT?
SALT.
CARROTS?
CARROTS.

CAT CAT!
CAT CAT.
...FOR A SOUP?

RUN!
RUN, RUN!
FOOD! HEH-HEH-HEH...

LUCIFEE MEAN. LUCIFEE SNEAKY.
WHAT DO NOW?
I'VE GOT IT!

IF WE CAN'T MAKE CINDERELLY FEEL BETTER, THEN WE'LL GO TO THE BALL FOR HER.

WE CAN DO IT! WE CAN DO IT! WE CAN HELP OUR CINDERELLY...

WHAT DO YOU THINK?
OH MY! IT'S VERY... WELL, IT'S CREATIVE, PERLA.

IT'S JUST NO USE. I'M GOING TO BE SICK FOR A SPELL...

DID YOU SAY SOMETHING ABOUT A "SPELL," MY DEAR?
YOU ALWAYS HAVE SUCH WONDERFUL TIMING!

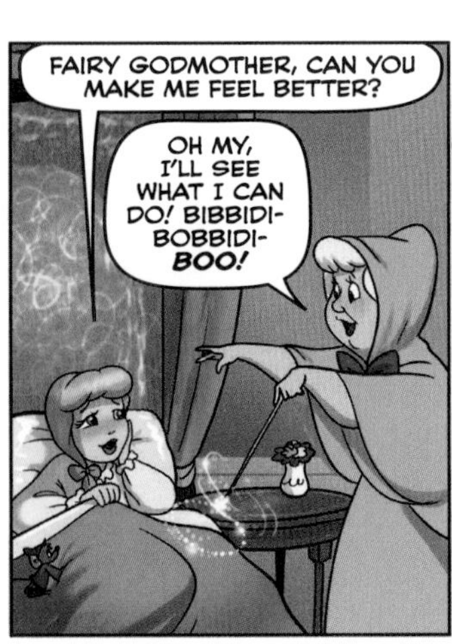

A GIFT TO REMEMBER

ANTSY GODMOTHER

I DON'T SEE ANY DEER, BUT IT'S HARD TO TELL FROM HERE.

PERHAPS THESE WILL HELP.

THANK YOU.

PLEASE TELL ME YOU'RE NOTICING THIS!
I'VE BEEN TRYING NOT TO ENCOURAGE IT.

"I SEE SOME DEER, BUT NOT THE ONE I SAW BEFORE.

"NOW WAIT JUST A MINUTE."

OH MY, THIS IS GETTING OUT OF HAND!

"OR OUT OF **WAND**, I SHOULD SAY!"

THERE'S REALLY NO NEED TO KEEP IMPROVING EVERYTHING.

I KNOW, IT'S JUST THAT I'M HERE TO MAKE EVERYTHING SO MAGICAL FOR YOU, BUT IT ALREADY IS!

AND THAT'S ALL THANKS TO YOU, BUT NOW MY LIFE IS PERFECT. YOU CAN RELAX, AND MAYBE TREAT YOURSELF TO A LITTLE MAGIC.
HMMM...

End

MY FAIR ROYAL HIGHNESS

GOOD AFTERNOON! IT'S SUCH A..**PLEASURE** TO BE HERE. LET'S GET THIS CIVIC COUNCIL MEETING UNDERWAY.

I LISTENED, DIDN'T I? YOU'D NEVER KNOW I WAS COMPLAINING ABOUT THE DUKE AND ALL HIS RIDICULOUS FOL-DE-ROL YESTERDAY!
NO ONE **WOULD** HAVE KNOWN...

...IF THE GRAND DUKE WASN'T SITTING RIGHT NEXT TO YOU.

MY DEAR GRAND DUKE! I FORGOT YOU WERE SITTING THERE, HOW DID THAT HAPPEN?
NO OFFENSE TAKEN, YOUR HIGHNESS. AFTER ALL...

...I CAN'T HELP THINKING THAT THESE MEETINGS MIGHT GO MORE SMOOTHLY **WITHOUT** YOUR ROYAL PRESENCE.
CINDERELLA! TELL HIM I'M A PERFECT DELIGHT!

THE NEXT MORNING...
AFTER YESTERDAY'S EVENTS, MAYBE I COULD OFFER SOME ADVICE ON BEING A MORE GRACIOUS MEETING ATTENDEE?

YOUNG LADY, I'VE BEEN A KING A LOT LONGER THAN YOU'VE BEEN A PRINCESS. I THINK I KNOW MORE ABOUT THESE THINGS THAN YOU DO.

WELL...LET'S SAY YOUR MIND WANDERED WHILE SOMEONE WAS TALKING. WHAT WOULD YOU DO?

EASY! I'D INTERRUPT AT ONCE AND START TALKING ABOUT MYSELF.
CLASS BEGINS NOW.

THE BEST WAY TO WELCOME YOUR COUNCIL MEMBERS IS TO ENGAGE THEM IN LIGHT CONVERSATION.

FOR INSTANCE...WHEN A COUNCILMAN MENTIONS A FAVORITE HOBBY, MAYBE YOU SHOULD ASK HIM A QUESTION ABOUT IT.
AH, I SEE...

WHEN A MAN TELLS ME HE COLLECTS RARE COINS, I MIGHT SAY, "HOW CAN YOU ENJOY SOMETHING SO INCREDIBLY DULL?"
LET'S START OVER AFTER LUNCH...

LATER...
YOUR GRACE!
I'D LIKE TO SEE THIS "EDUCATION" OF THE KING FOR MYSELF, IF I MAY.

I SEE, WELL--
I'VE ALWAYS LIKED THIS ROOM. SO MUCH NICER THAN THE OVERSTATED MESS HIS MAJESTY LIKES TO INHABIT.

THANK YOU, BUT, ER, I WOULDN'T SAY--
IT'S IMPOLITE TO INTERRUPT, YOUR HIGHNESS.

MAY I HAVE ANOTHER CHAIR FOR THE CLASS, PLEASE?

IT'S ESSENTIAL IN A POLITE CONVERSATION NOT TO INTERRUPT. LET'S TRY IT.

THE WEATHER HAS BEEN UNSEASONABLY WARM, DON'T YOU THINK?
YES, I--
IT HAS! HOWEVER--

THE SUN HAS BEEN GOOD FOR THE CROPS. DON'T YOU AGREE?
WELL, I--
IT HAS INDEED!

HOW FANTASTIC IT FEELS ***NOT*** TO BE INTERRUPTED!
QUITE SO! YOU SHOULD TRY IT SOMETIME, YOUR HIGHNESS.

RIBBON DUSTING

PRINCESS CHORES

STEPSISTERS

MY BIRTHDAY IS THREE DAYS AWAY SO YOU'D BETTER GET ME SOMETHING NICE THIS TIME, DRIZELLA.
NO USED HAIR RIBBONS OR STATIONERY YOU'VE ALREADY WRITTEN ON!
I RESENT THAT, ANASTASIA! I'M **VERY** GENEROUS.

WHY, I EVEN GAVE ***CINDERELLA*** A PRESENT FOR HER BIRTHDAY ONCE. DON'T YOU REMEMBER, CINDERELLA?

OH YES...YOU GAVE ME A CAKE OF LYE SO I COULD GET A CHOCOLATE STAIN OUT OF YOUR TAFFETA DRESS.
TRULY A GIFT FROM THE HEART!
End

BATH TIME

zZz
LUCIFER! IT'S TIME FOR YOUR BRUSHING!
zZz
LUCIFER! TIME FOR A TRIMMING!
LUCIFER! THERE'S A FRESH TROUT ON THE TABLE...
!
NOW YOU'RE AWAKE.
End

SNOW SPELLS

WOULD YOU DO ME THE HONOR OF JOINING ME FOR A HORSE-DRAWN CARRIAGE RIDE THROUGH THE FIRST SNOWFALL OF THE YEAR?

OH, DARLING, IT'S LIKE A FAIRY TALE!

I'LL JUST CHANGE INTO MY NEW TRAVELING DRESS! IT'S SO BEAUTIFUL AND WARM, LINED WITH--

IF ANYONE CAN FIX IT, YOU GIRLS CAN!
NO PROBLEMEY, CINDERELLY!

HOW IS IT COMING ALONG? DID YOU HAVE ANY LUCK?

OH. WHAT A LOVELY QUILT.
UH TOLDS YA! WUZ SPOSTA BE A ***PILLOW!***

SALADULA HIGGITY FIGGITUS, INCORPORUM ARBORETUM TANCAPITUS REMOLIUM FALLABELLA CRODISIUM INVINCICUS CAPARELLIUS...

INDISTERMIUM CALTERIMUS MORDIS PERTONIUS GARRASELLICKUM TANGENTIVAL PROSPONIBLE...

WHY SUCH A LONG SPELL?
WHEN IT'S THIS COLD OUT, IT'S IMPORTANT TO DRESS IN LAYERS!

SORRY THIS TOOK SO LONG. THERE WERE SOME... ALTERATIONS.

WOW! YOU LOOK BEAUTIFUL... DID THE MICE JUST WHIP THIS UP FOR YOU?

OH, THANK YOU! NO, THE CREDIT FOR ***THIS*** GOES TO FAIRY GODMOTHER.

THOUGH I HAD TO DRAW THE LINE AT THE GLASS SNOW BOOTS.
OOH.
End

Aurora

NATURE WALK

IT'S SUCH A LOVELY DAY, AND I HAVEN'T BEEN ON A WALK IN THE WOODS IN SO LONG.

NEITHER HAVE I! THAT'S A FANTASTIC IDEA!

LET ME JUST GET READY!

READY!
HOW FAR DID YOU PLAN ON WALKING?

LOOK AT THIS! WE DIDN'T EVEN NEED TO PACK A LUNCH.

WAIT! DON'T EAT THAT!
?

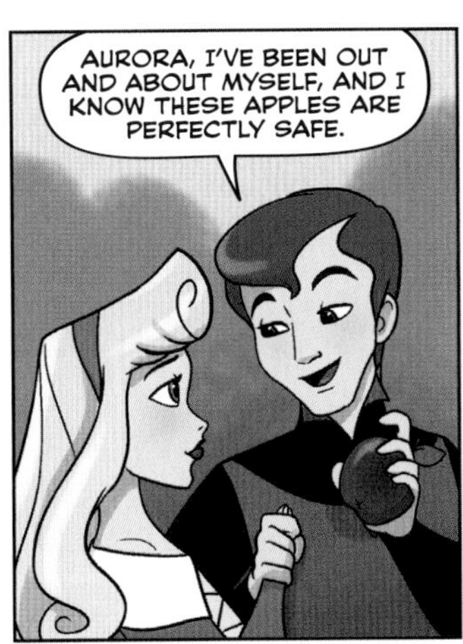
AURORA, I'VE BEEN OUT AND ABOUT MYSELF, AND I KNOW THESE APPLES ARE PERFECTLY SAFE.

I'M SURE THE WORM FELT THE SAME WAY.
BLORCH!

LISTEN! THAT'S A WHITE WAGTAIL. OVER THERE!

THEY'RE QUITE SHY.
BE GENTLE!

DON'T WORRY! IT SENSES I'M NOT A THREAT. PERHAPS MY GENTLE DEMEANOR.

OR THE COMPANY YOU KEEP?

THIS SPOT LOOKS NICE!

WHY DON'T WE MOVE A LITTLE MORE DOWN THE HILL.

BUT THE SHADE IS PERFECT HERE AND THERE'S NOTHING AROUND TO DISTURB US!

LIKE WE JUST DISTURBED THAT ANT COLONY?

BE CAREFUL. THOSE ROCKS CAN BE--

SPLASH
SLIPPERY.

I'M NOT USUALLY SO CLUMSY. I'M JUST NERVOUS, I SUPPOSE.
I KNOW. WE DANCE **BEAUTIFULLY,** MY DARLING.

WHILE YOU'RE IN THERE, THOUGH...

I FEEL SO STUPID. YOU WERE RAISED IN THESE WOODS, AFTER ALL...

BELIEVE IT OR NOT, UNLIKE EVERYONE ELSE IN THE CASTLE, I DID SPEND TIME IN THE FOREST.

IT'S ALL RIGHT, I'M JUST HAPPY TO HAVE SOMEONE TO SHARE ALL THIS WITH!

NEXT TIME WE JUST WON'T BRING HOME AS MANY NEW FRIENDS.
End

NEW FRIENDS

WET BOOTS

PRICELESS

EXPLORING THE CASTLE

WHAT'S WRONG, DEAR?

I'M JUST REALIZING HOW HUGE THIS CASTLE IS! I DON'T KNOW WHERE TO START EXPLORING.

WHY NOT THE BASEMENT? THEN WE CAN WORK OUR WAY UP! IT'S RIGHT THIS WAY!

NO NO, THE BASEMENT IS TO THE SOUTH.
WE'VE BEEN AWAY A WHILE, TOO, HAVEN'T WE?

IT'S SO DARK DOWN THERE. ARE YOU SURE IT'S SAFE?

NONSENSE! DARKNESS OR NOT, THIS IS YOUR HOME, WHERE YOU'RE ***PERFECTLY*** SAFE!

WHAT WAS THAT NOISE?
MERRYWEATHER'S HEART POUNDING.
I'M NOT SCARED. I'M JUST ***TERRIFIED!***

WHAT IS THAT ROOM?

I DON'T KNOW. WE HAVE NEVER VENTURED THIS FAR DOWN.

WANDS UP! WE DON'T WANT ANY SURPRISES!

FATHER?!?
WELL, THERE GOES THE LAST QUIET ROOM IN THE KINGDOM!
End

BIRTHDAY MAGIC

YOUR BIRTHDAY IS COMING UP, DEAR. ARE YOU EXCITED?

OH, FATHER INSISTS ON A BANQUET. I KNOW PHILLIP IS HIDING GIFTS IN THE STABLES, BUT...

I'D BE HAPPY WITH A HOMEMADE DRESS AND CAKE FROM MY FAVORITE FAIRIES. JUST LIKE THE OLD DAYS IN THE FOREST!

A SIMPLE BIRTHDAY! NO FRILLS OR RICHES OR MAGIC.
NO MAGIC?

OH DEAR! FLORA, MERRYWEATHER! LISTEN TO WHAT AURORA TOLD ME.

SHE WANTS A BIRTHDAY DRESS AND CAKE, LIKE WE DID ON HER 16TH BIRTHDAY. AND SHE WANTS IT ***WITHOUT*** MAGIC!

OH MY, WE NEVER ***DID*** TELL HER WE USED OUR WANDS . . .
WELL THEN, WE'LL DO IT ***RIGHT*** THIS TIME. NO MAGIC, FOR AURORA!

YOU... CHOP FOOD WITH THESE, RIGHT?
YES, AFTER YOU THREAD THE FORKS.

I FOUND THIS LOVELY SHADE OF FUCHSIA, AND I THOUGHT--
OH, NO! THAT'S JUST A FANCY WORD FOR ***PINK.***

WE CALL HER ***ROSE,*** SO PINK IS MOST APPROPRIATE!
SHE'S A PRINCESS, NOT A ***FLOWER!*** ROYAL BLUE!

OH, MERRY, LET'S NOT FIGHT AGAIN. SURELY WE CAN USE ***BOTH*** COLORS.
YES, WE JUST HAVE TO BE ***TASTEFUL.***

ARE YOU SURE THIS IS TASTEFUL?
IT'S A YOUNG PERSON'S TASTEFUL, DEAR.

I DECIDED TO KEEP IT SIMPLE THIS TIME.
AURORA

GOOD MORNING, PRINCESS.
HAPPY BIRTHDAY!!!
MY DARLINGS! THANK YOU!

WE MADE SOMETHING FOR YOU.
REALLY?! OH, SHOW ME!

!

WE DID OUR BEST, I'M SORR--
THEY'RE **BEAUTIFUL!!!!**

I CAN'T BELIEVE SHE'S WEARING OUR DRESS TO THE ***BANQUET!***
I CAN'T TELL IF PHILLIP'S HAPPY OR TRYING NOT TO LAUGH.

LOOK, HERE COMES THE CAKE...

WHY IS THE ***SERVANT*** EATING HER CAKE?
ROYAL TASTER, DEAR. IT'S HIS JOB.

BLEEEECH
WELL, THE ***FROSTING*** IS DELICIOUS.
End

FIRST SNOWFALL

HOW FAST DOES THIS GO?
LET'S FIND OUT!

AAAAAAHHHH!

LET'S GO AGAIN!
INCOMING!

IS THAT OUR COAT OF ARMS?!?
IF YOU'RE PLAYING IN THE SNOW, ALWAYS BRING A COAT!

LOOK! I MADE A SNOWMAN!

YOUR MAGIC DID MORE THAN THAT, FLORA.

OH MY!

AND NOW THE **BEST PART** OF A SNOW DAY!

I'M NOT SURE. AT OUR AGE, WE TIRE SO QUICKLY.
OUR AGE? SPEAK FOR YOURSELF! BUT I AGREE.

THEY'RE RIGHT. BESIDES, OUR CLOTHES ARE SOAKED THROUGH!
THAT'S WHY IT'S THE BEST PART!

HOT CHOCOLATE!
End

Ariel

SOMETHING TO SING ABOUT

AHHHH...NOPE! AH-AHHH?
SOUNDS LIKE ARIEL IS PRACTICING.

OH AHHH LA-LA-LA...NOPE!
BUT DAT'S NOT ANY SONG I EVER TAUGHT HER.

ARIEL, WHAT IS DAT YOU ARE SINGING?
I'M TRYING TO WRITE A SONG.

DERE IS NO TRY. AND RIGHT NOW, IT LOOKS LIKE "DO NOT."

I WANT TO WRITE SOMETHING THAT PEOPLE CAN ENJOY...

...BUT ALSO SING ALONG TO!

I WANT IT TO SPEAK TO THE HEART! THE SOUL!

WHAT'S IT ABOUT?
I HAVE NO IDEA.

ARIEL, A SONG MUSTN'T COME FROM THE LISTENER. IT HAS TO COME FROM ***YOU.***

TO SPEAK TO THE SOUL, IT HAS TO ***COME*** FROM THE SOUL!

NOW TELL ME, GIRL...WHAT INSPIRES YOUR PASSION FOR LIFE?

I FOUND ONE OF ***THESE!*** ISN'T IT ***NEAT?***
MARVELOUS.

LET'S TAKE A LOOK AT YOUR LYRICS.
"OOOOH YA-YAH, NO-NO, HEY-HEY. LA-LA-LA, YEAH-YEAH, WOO."

THE WOO IS UNDERLINED. LIKE "WOO!"
YES, I SEE DAT.

I WAS WORKING ON THE REFRAIN.

YES, WELL, YOU SHOULD REFRAIN FROM WRITING LYRICS LIKE DESE.

OKAY, I HAVE NEW LYRICS. TELL ME WHAT YOU THINK.

"I LOVE THE OCEAN, BUT I WANT TO TRAVEL. SEE BEYOND WHAT I KNOW, EXPLORE, BUT FATHER DOESN'T AGREE!"

MUCH BETTER! NOW WE JUST HAVE TO WORK ON RHYMING. AND RHYTHM.
WHAT ARE THOSE?

IT'S STRANGE, BECAUSE I KNOW YOU'VE LEARNED WHAT I TAUGHT YOU, BUT SOMEHOW... YOU DIDN'T.

TRY TO COUNT THE SYLLABLES IN EACH PHRASE. IF YOU GET THEM TO THE SAME NUMBER, THE SONG FLOWS BETTER-- THAT'S THE RHYTHM.

IF THE LAST SYLLABLE OF SOME LINES SOUND LIKE THE ONES AT THE ENDS OF OTHER LINES, DAT'S THE RHYME!

IT MAY BE HARD WORK, THE PROCESS IS LONG, BUT DAT IS THE WAY ONE MAKES UP A SONG!

MY LOVE OF THE OCEAN IS DEEP AND TRUE! LA-LA-LA-LA, LA-LA-LA-LA, LA-LA-LA-LA, WOO!
AT LEAST IT'S HONEST.
End

MUSIC CLASS

HEY, SEBASTIAN, CAN YOU DO ME A FAVOR?

I WANT TO PLAY ONE OF THOSE INSTRUMENTS!

BUT CHILD, YOUR VOICE IS SO BEAUTIFUL!
SURE, JUST LIKE MY SISTERS'.

BUT I WANT **MORE!**
YOU CAN'T REFRAIN FROM THAT OLD REFRAIN, CAN YOU?

FIRST THING WE NEED TO DO IS LEARN BASIC CHORDS.

THAT SHOULD BE EASY. THERE ARE ONLY SIX OF THEM.

NOT **THOSE** KIND OF CORDS. **MUSICAL** CHORDS! IT'S WHEN YOU PLAY SEVERAL STRINGS AT--

SWEET SEAWEED SYMPHONY! WHAT IS THIS NOISE?

WOW, THIS ONE HAS A LOT OF CORDS!

I **TOLD** YOU, CHILD, THESE ARE CALLED **STRINGS.** NOW PAY ATTENTION!

CHORDS ARE WHEN YOU HOLD SOME DOWN TO ADJUST THE SOUND, THEN PLAY THEM ALL AT ONCE!

ALL AT ONCE? THIS IS IMPOSSIBLE!
PERHAPS WE TRY THE FLUTE.

EACH OF THOSE HOLES CORRESPONDS TO A DIFFERENT TONE OF DA SCALE. ALL YOU HAVE TO DO IS--

WHAT NOTE IS THIS?
WELL, DEPENDING ON THE COMBINATION OF--

FWWWP!

I THINK IT'S BROKEN.
WELL, IT IS **NOW!**

THAT'S IT! YOU'VE GOT THE RHYTHM!
CHK CHK CHK

THWOK!
OW!
MAYBE NOT SO CLOSE NEXT TIME.

WOOWWWOWOWOO!
WHERE DID YOU EVEN FIND THIS?

WHAT'S THIS BUTTON DO?
I THINK MAYBE YOU'RE NOT READY FOR THIS ONE.

AHHH AH SUB MARI...
FLIP

...ET CHORO LUDENTIUM!

F!
End

TREASURE HUNT

WHAT THE PEOPLE KNOW

SAXOPHONE

WHAT THE WICK

SEBASTIAN, WHAT ARE YOU DOING HERE?
YOU ARE LATE TO REHEARSAL FOR DE SPRING CONCERT. AGAIN. THE PIKE WHO PLAYS FIFE SPOTTED YOU WERE HERE.

AND IF YOU PAID ATTENTION IN MUSIC CLASS, YOU WOULD KNOW DIS HAS GOT TO BE A MUSICAL INSTRUMENT. LISTEN,
CLEARLY, IT IS BROKEN.
YOU'RE CRAZY! HOW ARE YOU SUPPOSED TO MAKE MUSIC WITH A CLOTHES DRYER?

YOU KNOW WHAT I THINK IT IS? AN OBSTACLE COURSE FOR FISH!
WHAT ON EARTH ARE YOU TALKING ABOUT, MON?

WATCH ME JUMP IT!

UH, HOW ABOUT A LITTLE HELP HERE?
DIS WHOLE DAY JUST KEEPS GETTING STRANGER.

IT'S A CLOTHES DRYER, I TELL YA!
NO WAY! IT'S AN OBSTACLE COURSE.
IT'S GOT TO BE A MUSICAL INSTRUMENT!

LA LA LA

FA LA LA
IT'S A BACKSCRATCHER!
YEAH, LET'S GO WIT DAT.
YOU KNOW, THAT'S WHAT I THOUGHT IT WAS AT FIRST...

COME ON, ARIEL! WE'VE GOT TO GET YOU TO REHEARSAL DIS INSTANT!
DE BAND CHARGES WHETHER DEY PLAY OR NOT.
OKAY. OKAY.

THANK YOU, SCUTTLE!
SEE YA!
ANYTIME, ARIEL! ANYTIME.

WHAT A NICE GIRL. THE FISH IS CUTE, TOO.

Y'KNOW, I HATE TO SAY IT, BUT THE OTHER ONE'S A BIT OF A **CRAB.**

OH, ARIEL LEFT THIS HERE. I'VE GOTTA GET IT BACK TO HER!

!
KER-POW!

TOO BAD. A PERFECTLY GOOD FLIBBERBOBBIN RUINED BY THE ELEMENTS.
SPLOOSH!

I DON'T HEAR ANYTHING.
IT DOESN'T WORK.
IT'S BROKEN.
NO, YOU DON'T GET IT. YOU GOTTA LISTEN TO DE NOTES I'M ***NOT*** PLAYING.
End

MORNING SWIM

SHE NEVER MISSES HER MORNING SWIM.
I'M HEADING TO THE BEACH, ERIC. BACK IN A BIT!
YOU COULD LEARN SOMETHING FROM HER, SIRE. EXERCISE IS IMPORTANT!

THE BEST PART OF MY MORNING IS GETTING TO SEE THE TWO OF YOU!

AND IT'S ABSOLUTELY WORTH THE MANY LEAGUES WE HAVE TO SWIM TO REACH YOU.

DON'T WORRY ABOUT HIM--SEBASTIAN'S IN THE BEST SHAPE HE'S EVEN BEEN.
I CAN PLAY THE CONGA UNTIL THE DANCERS ARE THE ONES BEGGING FOR A BREAK!
End

THINKAP

TODAY I'M GONNA TELL YA ABOUT THIS LITTLE NUMBER.

THIS IS CALLED A THINKAP! Y'SEE, HUMANS DO A LOTTA THINKING...

SO ONCE IN A WHILE THEY WEAR ONE-A THESE TO COLLECT AAALL THOSE THOUGHTS FOR SAFE-KEEPIN'!

HOW YA DOIN', SWEETIE?
I NEED ANOTHER THINKAP; THIS ONE'S FULL...
ERIC
ERIK
ERIC
End

PUNS

HEY, ARIEL..
NO...

WHAT'S A MERMAID'S FAVORITE NOTE TO SING?
NOOOOOO...

MIDDLE C!
UUUGGH, THAT'S TERRIBLE!

SEBASTIAN THOUGHT SO, TOO. HE'S A REAL CRAB, THAT ONE...
OH PLEASE MAKE IT STOP...
End

BUOY OH BUOY

End

SUNKEN TREASURE

FLOUNDER! COME HERE! I'VE FOUND A MAP!

LOOK, THERE ARE MONSTERS AND SERPENTS AND A BIG STAR ON IT.
THOSE DON'T LOOK LIKE ANYTHING DOWN HERE.

I KNOW. THEY MUST BE LAND CREATURES!

FROM THIS MYSTERIOUS ISLAND CALLED "X"! WE GOTTA FIND IT!

I'VE SEEN HUMANS HOLD THESE OUT IN FRONT OF THEIR BOATS, BUT WHY?

HUH?
NO, LOOK, THEY STAND LIKE THIS.

PRFFT!
?!
!?

MAYBE IT BREAKS WHEN THEY REACH LAND?
YOU'D THINK THEY JUST USE THEIR ***EYES...***

WHATEVER IS IN HERE MUST BE ***REALLY*** IMPORTANT!

UGH!

WOOOOW, WE HIT THE JACKPOT, FLOUNDER! IS THAT WHAT I THINK IT IS...?

I GOT A ***JAR OF DIRT!!***
WHOA, DON'T DROP IT!

End

OAK ISLAND

OOH! A CAVE!

YOU NEVER CAN GUESS WHAT YOU'LL FIND, ONLY THAT IT'S GOING TO BE SOMETHING SPECIAL!

MAYBE SOMETHING NEW, OR SOMETHING OLD AND LOST...

...OR MAYBE A DEAD END.

I THINK I HEAR SOMETHING!

I JUST HAVE TO KNOW WHAT'S ON THE OTHER SIDE!

YIPES!

CAP'N! THE HOLE IS FLOODING!
THE ISLAND IS SINKING!

WE NEED TO STOP THE FLOODING OR WE'LL LOSE THE TREASURE!

WE CAN LAY DOWN SOME PLANKS TO HOLD IT BACK!

THERE! THAT SHOULD DO IT.

I'M SORRY ABOUT FLOODING YOUR TREASURE.
GAH!

DID YOU SEE THAT?
METHINKS IT WAS A MERMAID!
AND SHE SAW OUR STOLEN TREASURE!

FILL IT WITH SAND AND LAY DOWN MORE PLANKS! WE CAN TRAP HER WITH THAT TREASURE!

THEN WE CAN PROTECT THE REST OF THE GOLD THAT WE'RE BURYING OVER THERE!

HELLO!
AHH! CAP'N!

IT'S CLEAR THE MERMAID IS TAUNTING US, MEN. OAK ISLAND IS CURSED!

BEST WE LEAVE NOW. WE CAN RETURN FOR OUR TREASURE ANOTHER DAY.

IT SOUNDS LIKE THEY'RE JUST LEAVING ALL THIS BEHIND.

MAYBE THEIR TREASURE IS CURSED!

THAT'S SILLY. THESE ARE JUST THINGS, AND NOW THEY CAN'T GET TO THEM. THIS IS MY FAULT.

I KNOW HOW I CAN HELP! BUT IT'LL REQUIRE A LOT OF DIGGING!

LUCKILY, WE KNOW WHERE EVERYTHING IS BURIED.
THREE SEPARATE BATCHES OF TREASURE, SO EVEN IF SOMEONE FINDS ONE, THEY'LL NEVER FIND IT ALL!

THANK GOODNESS FOR THESE TUNNELS! THERE! ALL IN ONE BIG, NEW PLACE!

End

SHARK DREAMS

DO YOU EVER CHASE THE FLOATING ISLANDS?
I DON'T THINK I'VE EVER SEEN ONE.

THEY'RE BIG AND AND HAVE BOOMING TUBES AND LITTLE CREATURES AND FLAGS.
OH, I THINK YOU MEAN "SHIPS".

I MAKE FRIENDS WITH THEM PRETTY EASILY. I THINK BECAUSE OF MY SMILE.
REALLY?

OH, SURE. WHEN THEY SEE ME, THEY YELL ***"CHUM!"*** AND THROW ME SOME LUNCH!

DO YOU EVER WANT TO SWIM UP WHEN IT'S DARK TO THOSE LANTERN FISH THEY HAVE?
WELL AT NIGHT, I'M USUALLY--OH, RIGHT. SORRY.

I'VE NEVER SEEN ANY LANTERN FISH, THOUGH.
THEY'RE WAY DEEP UP THERE, LIKE OURS ARE WAY DOWN DEEP HERE.

EVERY NIGHT THEY LINE UP THE SAME WAY AND MOVE ACROSS THE SKY. THEY FORM SHAPES AND PICTURES, AND SOME OF THEM JUST ZIP ALONG REALLY FAST.

I THINK THOSE ARE CALLED "STARS."
I'VE SEEN STARFISH. THEY DON'T TWINKLE.

WELL, I SHOULD GET GOING. I NEED TO REST A LITTLE. IT'S BEEN A PLEASURE!

I THOUGHT YOU SAID YOU COULDN'T SLEEP.

NO, BUT SOMETIMES I LET THE CURRENTS THAT RUN ALONG THE LAND DO MOST OF THE SWIMMING FOR ME.

THAT'S WHY THEY CALL IT THE ***COAST!***

End

HOMEWORK

ARIEL, I SEE YOU ARE KEEPING UP ON YOUR HOMEWORK?

I AM! LOOK! I'M MAKING A MAP!

AND YOU EXPLORED THE AREAS I ASSIGNED?
OF COURSE! WHY?

BECAUSE "HERE THERE BE" NO MONSTERS ***I'VE*** EVER SEEN.

I THOUGHT SOME MONSTERS WOULD MAKE THE MAP INTRIGUING!

THE POINT OF THESE ASSIGNMENTS IS TO EDUCATE YOU, FILL YOUR HEAD WITH WHAT YOU'LL NEED TO GET BY IN LIFE.

BUT WHAT IF WHAT I NEED IN LIFE IS ADVENTURE?

YOU DON'T SEE MY PROBLEM AS A PROBLEM, DO YOU?

THERE WAS SO LITTLE OUT THERE TO LOOK AT. I HAD TO DRAW ***SOMETHING!***

THERE WAS NOTHING BUT ROCKS AND CORAL AND MORE ROCKS.

THOSE BORING ***DETAILS*** ARE ***MARKERS*** SO PEOPLE DON'T GET LOST.

HOW CAN ANYONE DISCOVER SOMETHING NEW IF THEY DON'T GET LOST LOOKING?
BY BORROWING SOMEONE ELSE'S MAP.

MAYBE CARTOGRAPHY ISN'T YOUR STRONG SUIT. DID YOU DISCOVER ANY PLANT LIFE?

I DID! I SAW SOMETHING LIKE SEAWEED, BUT BLUISH PURPLE! AND IT WAS THICK!

IT WAS DRIFTING UP, THEN WAVING AROUND...
AND WHAT IS IT CALLED?

I DON'T KNOW, SO I NAMED IT "TWILIGHT DANCEGRASS"!
IT'S CALLED LAVER.

DID YOU SEE ANY INTERESTING ANIMALS WHILE YOU WERE OUT?

A STAR DRAGON! IT LOOKED LIKE A COLOSSAL SEA HORSE WITH STARFISH SKIN!

AND IT WAS HUGE! WHEN IT SWUNG ITS TAIL, THE ***TIDES CHANGED!***

DID YOU REALLY SEE THAT?
NO, JUST A WHALE LOOKING FOR EXOTIC PLANKTON.

I WAS HOPING YOU WOULD FIND SOMETHING THAT INSPIRED YOU TO LEARN. YOU'RE SMART, BUT RARELY APPLY YOURSELF TO YOUR EDUCATION.

AT LEAST TOMORROW I KNOW YOU'LL GIVE YOUR ALL FOR SEBASTIAN'S MUSIC CLASS.

OH! WE'RE LEARNING A NEW SONG ABOUT AN OCTOPUS! HIS EIGHT ARMS LINE UP WITH THE EIGHT NOTES IN THE SCALE!

I HAVE TO READ UP ON THEM SO I CAN DO THE PIECE JUSTICE.
SO YOU--
SHH! PLEASE! LEARNING!
End

Belle

BELLE'S DILEMMA

MAM'SELLE, WHY YOU ALWAYS SIT IN *ZIS* CHAIR? WE 'AVE SO MANY!
WELL, I LIKE IT BECAUSE IT'S... PRIVATE.

CACHÉ, MAM'SELLE?
OH I JUST MEAN THAT... WELL...

WHEN YOU LIVE WITH ENCHANTED OBJECTS THAT CAN HEAR AND SEE EVERYTHING YOU DO, SOMETIMES YOU NEED SOME... TIME ALONE, YOU KNOW?
OUI OUI, I UNDERSTAND ***ABSOLUMENT!***

EVERYBODY OUT! *TOUT DE SUITE!*
AWWW...
'SCUSE ME, MISS, YOU'RE ON MY TASSELS.

AHH, FINALLY SOME PEACE AND PRIVACY...

AH!
'ULLO!

I DON'T BELIEVE THIS, AN ENCHANTED **BOOKMARK?**
KEEP GOING, YOU'RE NEARLY AT THE BIT WHERE--

I'LL TAKE THAT, CHILD, YOU JUST RELAX.

ALLOW ME! GOOD NIGHT, MISS BELLE.
ER... THANK YOU.

SO, TONIGHT YOU WILL BE WEARING THIS LOVELY YELLOW PEIGNOIR WITH THE FINEST SPANISH LACE...

I HOPE MY **DREAMS** AREN'T PICKED FOR ME...
AND NOW, THE QUARTET WILL PLAY 'PERSIAN DREAMSCAPE'

I NEED TO TALK TO YOU.
WHA?

I DON'T MEAN TO SOUND RUDE, BECAUSE I **KNOW** EVERYONE MEANS WELL...
WHAT HAPPENED?

I JUST...DON'T NEED EVERYTHING DONE **FOR** ME! IT'S DRIVING ME CRAZY!
I'M NOT SURE I--

I WENT TO SCRATCH MY NOSE. LUMIERE TRIED TO HELP AND ALMOST SCORCHED MY HAIR!
I'LL TALK TO THEM.

I WANT TO POLITELY REMIND EVERYONE THAT BELLE DOES NOT NEED ATTENDING TO **ALL** OF THE TIME. IN FACT, SHE FINDS IT A BIT STIFLING.

WELL! HOW UNGRATEFUL. WE'RE TREATING HER LIKE A **PRINCESS.**
BUT SHE EEZ **NOT** A PRINCESS, SHE EEZ NOT USED TO ZIS ATTENTION!

I CAN'T LET THE POOR CHILD **WORK**, SHE'S NOT A SERVANT!
DO YOU **WANT** A TRUE LOVE WITH ROUGH, CHAPPED HANDS, SIRE?

WHY ON **EARTH** WOULD I CARE ABOUT **THAT??**
GOOD POINT, SIRE, CONSIDERING SHE DOESN'T SEEM TO MIND YOUR... AROMA.

NO NO NO...!
THERE IS **PROTOCOL** TO OBSERVE!
WE'RE JUST DOING OUR JOB!
GRRRR...

SILENCE!
WHAM

SHLUMPNFLORCH

OH NO, HER **BOOKS...**
OOOH, CHAUCER IS HEAVY!

ENCHANTED ADJUSTMENTS

LATE NIGHT READS

BELLE FEAST

THE END

BEAUTY AND THE BOOKS

YOU HAVE SO MANY FAIRY TALES HERE!

HMMM...HOW DO I SORT THEM? BY DISTANCE OF KINGDOMS? EPIC LEVEL OF SWORD FIGHTS? CHARMINGNESS OF PRINCES?

DONE!
UMMM...HOW EXACTLY DID YOU SORT THEM?

I PUT ALL THE ONES WITH HAPPY ENDINGS HERE.

MINE ARE IN ORDER FROM TALLEST TO SHORTEST.

I SORTED MINE BY COLOR, DEAR.

I THOUGHT IT BEST TO PLACE THE UGLIEST ONES SO THAT NOBODY CAN SEE THEM.
HMMM...

I LOVE IT! IT CAN BE OUR "MYSTERY PICK" SECTION!

I DECLARE THIS LIBRARY ***ORGANIZED!*** GREAT WORK, EVERYBODY.

BIOGRAPHIES ARE OVER ON THE SOUTH WALL AND ADVENTURE STORIES ARE HIGH UP HERE, NEARLY OUT OF REACH.
IT'S ***PERFECT!***

AND I MADE THIS SHELF JUST FOR YOU.
WHAT'S THIS SECTION?

ANGER MANAGEMENT.
YES'M.
End

TWELFTH NIGHT

BEAST POETRY

ROMEO AND JULIET

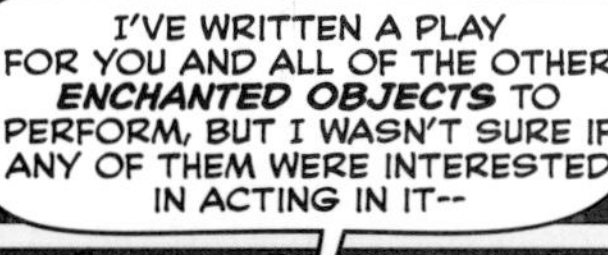
STAGE STRUCK

I'VE WRITTEN A PLAY FOR YOU AND ALL OF THE OTHER **ENCHANTED OBJECTS** TO PERFORM, BUT I WASN'T SURE IF ANY OF THEM WERE INTERESTED IN ACTING IN IT--

WHOOSH

ER...I **THINK** IT'S SAFE TO SAY THEY'RE **INTERESTED.**

YOU KNOW, I'D BE **HAPPY** TO SUPPLY ALL OF THE **COSTUMES** FOR THE PLAY.
WELL, MOST OF THE ENCHANTED OBJECTS ARE **TOO SMALL** TO WEAR COSTUMES.

I'M SURE I CAN FIND **SOMETHING** FOR THEM TO WEAR.
HOW ABOUT THIS ONE?
NOPE, SORRY.

MOMENTS LATER...
HOW ABOUT THIS ONE?
NOPE!

LATER STILL...
THIS ONE?
NOPE.
SIGH...

OKAY EVERYONE, FROM THE TOP!
WAIT...

WE CAN'T BEGIN REHEARSAL YET.
WHY NOT?

ER...IT'S LUMIÈRE.
IS HE SICK?
NOT "SICK," SO MUCH AS "IN LOVE"...

...WITH **HIMSELF.**
WHO IS THE MOST **HANDSOME** CANDELABRA **IN THE ENTIRE WORLD?**

BE OUR GUEST, BE OUR GUEST...

PUT OUR SERVICE TO THE TEST...
UM...LUMIÈRE...

WHAT'S WRONG, BELLE? AREN'T I GIVING A GOOD PERFORMANCE?
OH, YOU DEFINITELY **ARE,** IT'S JUST THAT...

...YOU'RE NOT PERFORMING **MY PLAY.**
OOPS.

AH, THE SCARLET CANDELABRA! GOOD TO SEE YOU!
YES, 'TIS I!!

GOOD JOB EVERYONE, BUT JUST BE **CAREFUL.**
"CAREFUL" ABOUT WHAT?
YOU DON'T WANT TO BE **TOO LOUD!**
OH COME ON, WHO WOULD NOT LOVE TO HEAR...

...THE **DULCET TONES** OF MY **BOOMING VOICE??**
GRRRRR...

WHAT'S WRONG?
YOU'RE ALL DOING A WONDERFUL JOB WITH YOUR PLAY, BUT I WAS WONDERING IF YOU COULD REHEARSE JUST A LITTLE BIT MORE...QUIETLY.

QUIETLY? **QUIETLY??** WE'RE TOO LOUD? THIS IS OUTRAGEOUS, AND I FOR ONE WILL NOT STAND HERE--

GRRRRR....

YOU KNOW, NOW THAT I THINK OF IT, WE **WERE** BEING TOO LOUD!

TOUGH CHOICES

TUMBLEWEEDS

MAY I ASK WHEN THE WEST WING WAS LAST DUSTED?
DUSTED?

I...THINK A FEW CORNERS MAY HAVE BEEN MISSED.

HOW–?
WELL MASTER, YOU **DO** HAVE A TENDENCY TO SHED...
End

UNWIND

SO YOU REALLY MANAGE ***EVERYTHING*** IN THE CASTLE, COGSWORTH?
OH, THE LIST IS ***ENDLESS,*** MADEMOISELLE.

THE HALLWAYS MUST BE DUSTED, DINNER MUST BE ON TIME AND THE SERVANTS NEED CONSTANT INSTRUCTING AND ORDERING!

EVEN ***YOU,*** LUMIERE?
OH YES....

OBEYING HIM, ON THE OTHER HAND...
THIS IS WHY I CAN'T UNWIND!
End

FIGHTING UTENSILS

THE SILVERWARE IS AT IT AGAIN...
THE PLATES AREN'T SPEAKING TO THE TEASPOONS AND THE FORKS CAN'T STAND TO BE NEXT TO EACH OTHER.

WHAT IF WE PUT THE SALAD FORKS ***ABOVE*** THE PLATES, INSTEAD? THEY WOULDN'T FIGHT, THEN...
GASP

OH MY, IS HE ALL RIGHT?
OH, YES. IF ZE TABLE SETTING IS ***WRONG,*** HE PASSES OUT.
MY TICKER...!
End

GASTON'S BOOK CLUB

BEEF CAKE

DISGUISE

MOGNIPICENK

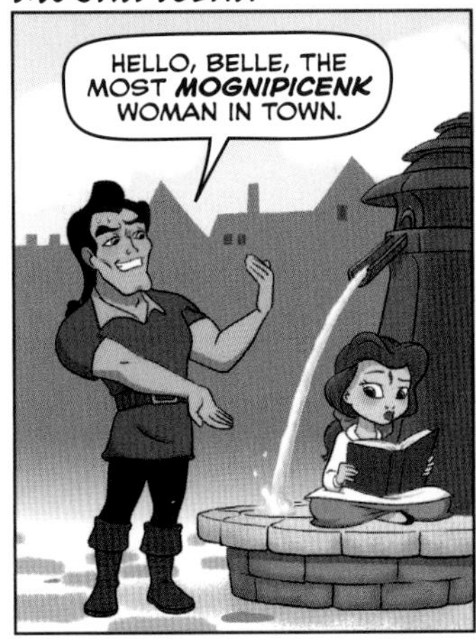

BELLE & MAURICE

SAUCY INVENTION

BEASTLY

I TELL YOU, LUMIÈRE, THAT BLASTED MONGREL HAS GOTTEN ON MY LAST NERVE!
IT TRACKS MUD ACROSS THE CARPETS, CHASES THE THROW PILLOWS...

AH, OUI, MON AMI! BUT AT LEAST YOU ARE ARE NOT ZE PREFERRED CHEW TOY!

EXACTLY! IT'S TIME SOMETHING WAS DONE ABOUT THAT UNRULY BEAST!
WHO, ME?

ROWF ROWF ROWF!

AAAAA!

SNARRRL!

I'M SURE THERE'S A GREAT STORY THERE...
End

INSOMNIA

I DON'T KNOW WHY, BUT I JUST CAN'T GET TO SLEEP.

MAYBE SOME LIGHT READING WILL HELP.

NOW WHAT?

IT'S SUCH A LOVELY NIGHT.

AND THE MOON IS FULL AND BEAUTIFUL!

≥SIGH≤ IS AN ECLIPSE TOO MUCH TOO ASK?

CAN'T SLEEP, MY DEAR?
UNFORTUNATELY NOT.

IT HAPPENS TO ME ALL THE TIME.

I THINK IT'S BECAUSE I CARRY AROUND TEA ALL DAY. ALL OF THAT CAFFEINE!

HAVE YOU CONSIDERED CHAMOMILE TEA?
THE MASTER LIKES HIS TEA TO HAVE BITE.

I HEARD VOICES. IT SEEMS I'M NOT THE ONLY ONE WHO CAN'T SLEEP.

WE'VE BEEN TRYING TO THINK OF ANYTHING TO HELP.

WE COULD TRY COUNTING SHEEP!

I'M A CLOCK. ALL I DO ALL DAY IS KEEP COUNT.

I OVERHEARD YOU DISCUSSING COUNTING SHEEP. ALLOW ME TO HELP.

I HAVE BEEN AT THE WINDOW ALL NIGHT. THERE ARE NO SHEEP AS FAR AS I COULD SEE.

I LIKE TO KEEP A LIGHT FOR THE MASTER ON THE DARKEST OF NIGHTS.
BUT IT'S A BIG, BRIGHT FULL MOON TONIGHT.

I LIKE TO KEEP IN PRACTICE?

I HEARD EVERYONE TALKING. IS SOMETHING WRONG?
EVERYTHING IS FINE. WE JUST CAN'T SLEEP.

AND BY THE LOOK ON YOUR FACE, WE ALL HAVE TO BE UP SOON ANYWAY.
THE LOOK ON MY FACE IS EXHAUSTION.

SHE IS CORRECT. DAWN APPROACHES, AND WE HAVE OUR CHORES TO START ON.
I JUST HOPE WE HAVE THE ENERGY.

End

ENDINGS

BELLE?

WHAT'S WRONG?
OH...I JUST FINISHED MY BOOK.

I'M SORRY, WAS IT THAT BAD?
NO...

IT WAS THAT GOOD!
End

Jasmine

WORLD OF RAIN

VIEW FROM THE TOP

CARPET SALE

BIRTHDAY WISH

HAPPY BIRTHDAY!

THESE GIFTS ARE FROM ME, OF COURSE.
FATHER, YOU SHOULDN'T HAVE!

YOU DON'T LIKE THEM?

IT'LL TAKE ME UNTIL MY NEXT BIRTHDAY TO FIND OUT.

HERE! I SAW THIS, AND THOUGHT YOU WOULD LOVE IT, SO I PICKED IT UP RIGHT AWAY.

DEFINE "PICKED UP."
I PAID FOR IT, FAIR AND SQUARE!

WELL IT'S ABSOLUTELY PERFECT. THANK YOU.

OH, THANK YOU, TOO, ABU. NOW I HAVE TWO OF THEM.
NO, IT'S THE SAME ONE.

ON THIS MOMENTOUS OCCASION OF TURNING--ACTUALLY, I WON'T ASK, IT'S NEVER POLITE, BUT HOWEVER OLD YOU ARE, SUBTRACT THREE, YOU LOOK GREAT--

--ANYWAY, I HUMBLY GRANT YOU ONE BIRTHDAY WISH. ANYTHING YOUR HEART DESIRES!

THAT'S A THING? MY BIRTHDAY IS NEXT MONTH!

JUST FOR HER. I'M STILL NOT SURE YOU HAVE A HEART. JUST DESIRES.

SO WHAT'LL IT BE? A PONY? AN ARMY? A PONY ARMY? WOULDN'T THAT LOOK CUTE MARCHING INTO WAR... NOT REALLY YOUR STYLE.

HOW ABOUT A NONMAGIC LAMP? IT GRANTS THE WISH OF LIGHT, AND THAT'S ABOUT IT. AND A YEAR'S SUPPLY OF LAMP OIL!

THANK YOU, BUT I ALREADY HAVE PLENTY IN MY LIFE TO KEEP ME HAPPIER THAN I'D EVER DREAMED.

DON'T LOOK A WISH HORSE IN THE MOUTH.

EVERYONE HAS ALREADY BEEN SO GENEROUS AND THOUGHTFUL WITH THEIR GIFTS.

WELL, EXCEPT ABU.

A GIFT SHOULD BE SOMETHING FROM THE HEART, FROM ONE PERSON TO ANOTHER. AND I'VE TRIED TO EARN AND DESERVE ALL OF THE THINGS THAT MAKE MY LIFE GREAT, INSTEAD OF JUST WISHING FOR THEM.

YOU UNDERSTAND, RIGHT?
HOW ABOUT THIS? I'D SAY YOU EARNED IT.
I survived the Cave of Wonders and all I got was this shirt.

I DIDN'T KNOW WHAT TO GET YOU. I NEVER DO. PEOPLE TELL ME. IT'S SORT OF MY WHOLE THING.

I'M SORRY. I DO APPRECIATE IT. HOW'S THIS--I WISH WE COULD ALL HAVE A NICE, QUIET DINNER TOGETHER.
DONE!

THIS IS AMAZING! YOU'RE USING THE BREAD AS A BOWL!
MY WISH IS TO NOT HAVE TO DO THE DISHES.
End

QUEEN FOR A DAY

SINCE I'M UNDER THE WEATHER, JASMINE, YOU'LL HAVE TO RULE IN MY PLACE...
...FOR TODAY, ANYWAY!
O-OKAY, FATHER.

YOU'LL SIT ON THE THRONE AND ATTEND TO ALL MY BUSINESS MATTERS.
OF COURSE!

OH, AND ONE OTHER THING...
YES?

TELL ABU TO GET OFF OF ME!
HE'S JUST TRYING TO GIVE YOU A SOOTHING MASSAGE...

8:00 A.M.
CONSIDER THIS ROYAL PROCLAMATION SIGNED!

8:30 A.M.
AND CONSIDER THIS OTHER ROYAL PROCLAMATION SIGNED!

9:00 A.M.
...AND CONSIDER THIS OTHER--
--HEY, WHERE'D THE PROCLAMATION GO?

YOU'RE JUST AS BORED AS I AM, AREN'T YOU, RAJAH?

WAIT A MINUTE! I'M THE QUEEN!
FOR TODAY, ANYWAY. THAT MEANS...
...I CAN MAKE ROYAL DECREES.

I DECREE THAT TODAY IS "FEED THE QUEEN AN APPLE WHENEVER SHE WANTS ONE" DAY!

YES, MY QUEEN!
AT ONCE, MY QUEEN!
!

IT'S GOOD TO BE THE QUEEN!

CARPET, ARE THERE ANY MORE APPLES?

WHOOSH

HEY, WHAT ARE YOU--?

SEE, RAJAH? THIS JOB DOESN'T **HAVE** TO BE BORING!

WHAT **ELSE** CAN YOU JUGGLE, CARPET?

WOW!

UM, CARPET, I DON'T KNOW IF THAT'S A GOOD IDEA--
WHOMP

WELL, **THAT'S** WHAT HAPPENS WHEN YOU MESS WITH RAJAH.

HMM, **WHAT ELSE** COULD I DO FOR ENTERTAINMENT UNTIL MY FATHER FEELS BETTER?

WELL, ASK A SILLY QUESTION...

SOMETHING COLD

MYSTERY CAVE

SO...WHY ARE WE WALKING **TOWARD** THE DARK, UNKNOWN HOLE?
COME ON, WHAT ARE CAVES **FOR** BUT TO BE EXPLORED?

GREAT. SO WE'RE JUST GONNA WANDER **RIGHT** ON IN?
THAT'S THE PLAN!

YER NOT EVEN **REMOTELY** WORRIED ABOUT WHAT MIGHT BE **IN** HERE ALREADY?
WHAT ABOUT **SAFETY,** JASMINE?

I BROUGHT **THIS!**
THAT'S IT, I'M STICKIN' WITH THE CAT...

C'MON IAGO, WHERE'S YOUR SENSE OF ADVENTURE?
I HAVE **PLENTY** OF ADVENTURE! IT'S THE **RECKLESS ENDANGERMENT** I DON'T LIKE!

THERE! SEE? THE CAT IS SNIFFING, WHY IS THE CAT SNIFFING??
sniff
sniff

GRRRRRRRRRRR...
AND NOW THE GROWLING! I'M NOT GOIN' **ANY** FARTHER.

OKAY, YOU CAN STAY HERE IN THE DARK!
WAIT FOR ME!

RAJAH?? WOW, HE JUST RAN OFF!
SEE? YA LET AN INDOOR CAT GO OUTSIDE AND BOOM, THEY'RE GONE!

IAGO, LESS COMPLAINING, MORE FINDING MY TIGER!
WHY ARE WE EVEN **IN** HERE?

THE LAST DUST STORM REVEALED THIS CAVE. IT'S NOT IN ANY PALACE RECORDS, SO I'M GOING TO SURVEY IT AND ADD IT!

WELL IF THE CAVE STARTS TELLING US NOT TO **TOUCH** ANYTHING, **THEN** CAN WE LEAVE?
FAIR ENOUGH.

THIS WHOLE THING SMELLS LIKE A TRAP!
ACTUALLY, I SMELL PLANTS. THAT'S IMPOSSIBLE, NOTHING COULD GROW IN THIS DARKNESS..
sniff sniff

PLANTS?? LIKE BITTER ALMONDS? AAAH, POISON--
IAGO, CALM DOWN.

HONESTLY, WHAT A FUSSPOT. YOU'RE PROBABLY SCARIER THAN ANYTHING IN HERE.
I'LL JUST BE UNDER HERE 'TIL WE'RE HOME.

I HAVEN'T SEEN ANY WARNINGS OF TRAPS, SO I DON'T THINK THERE'S ANYTHING TOO VALUABLE IN HERE.

WAIT! DO YOU HEAR THAT NOISE?

SO WE'RE JUST GONNA IGNORE THE GROWLING PART?
RRRRRRRRRRRRR...

YOU CAUSE A DISTRACTION WHILE I GET MY TIGER.
HOOOOOLD UP, ARE YOU IMPLYING I'M LOUD?

RAJAH? HERE RAJ--

AAAAH!!!
IAGO!

RAJAH, YOU'VE FOUND A SPICE HOARD! SOME OF THESE PLANTS ARE EXTINCT! GOOD KITTY!
NOOOO, NOT THE CATNIP!
PURRRRRRRRRR...

End

CAT NAP

A HOT ARABIAN NIGHT.

GOOD RAJAH. THERE'S YOUR TIGER PILLOW, RIGHT OVER THERE.

OOOF! NO, RAJAH, DOWN. TIGER PILLOW! TIGER PILLOW!

I CAN'T FEEL MY LEGS!!
PURRRR...

RAJAH, YOU ARE TOO HEAVY TO SLEEP ON MY LEGS.
PURRRR...

LOOK, RAJAH. A BIRDIE!
RAWWWR?

GO GET IT!

PURRRR...
OKAY. PLEASE GET IT?

RAJAH, NO PLAYING. SLEEP.

IF YOU WANT TO STAY UP HERE, SETTLE DOWN.

OKAY, THAT'S BETTER. WE CAN SHARE THE BED. SHARE...

TEN MINUTES LATER.
FIRST THING TOMORROW, I WILL FIND A NEW TIGER TRAINER.

JASMINE?

JASMINE? JASMINE, WHERE ARE MY SPARE TURBAN FEATHERS? LET ME REMIND YOU THEY ARE NOT TIGER TOYS--

JASMINE?! RAJAH, WHAT'S THAT IN YOUR MOUTH?
?

YOU ATE MY JASMINE?!
HOW CAN I SLEEP WITH ALL THIS NONSENSE?

WHILE JASMINE SLEEPS OUTSIDE...
GUARDS! GUARDS!!!
GRRR?

RAJAH, I COMMAND YOU TO OPEN YOUR MOUTH AT ONCE!
?

DEAREST? ARE YOU IN THERE?
RAAWWWR... RAAWWWWWR!

POOR JASMINE. SHE'S GONE ABSOLUTELY FERAL.
???

THE SULTAN THINKS RAJAH ATE PRINCESS JASMINE!
RAJAH, I ORDER YOU TO COUGH UP THE PRINCESS THIS INSTANCE.

DID YOU HEAR ME, YOU GROWLING PILE OF PILLOWS? COUGH HER UP NOW!
GRRRRRR!

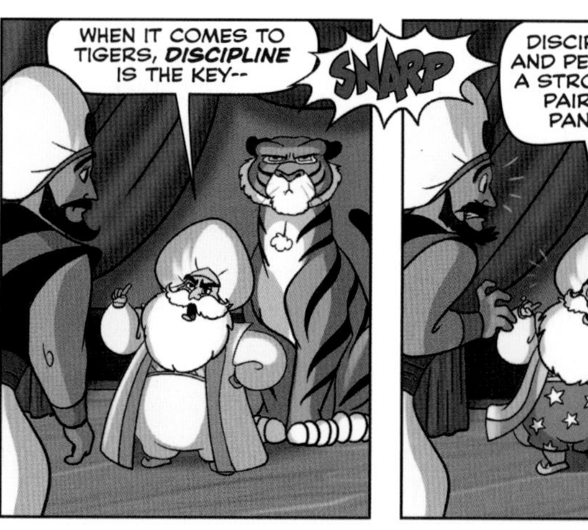
WHEN IT COMES TO TIGERS, DISCIPLINE IS THE KEY--
SNARP
DISCIPLINE, AND PERHAPS A STRONGER PAIR OF PANTS.

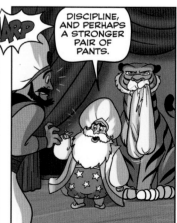

COUGH UP MY DAUGHTER, YOU BEAST!
GRRROWWWR!

WOULD YOU PLEASE KEEP THE NOISE DOWN? I'M TRYING TO SLEEP!

THANK YOU!

WELL, I... SUPPOSE WE'RE **ALL** A LITTLE TO BLAME HERE, RIGHT RAJAH?
GRRRR!

ZZZZ...

SIGHHHH...

THERE'S ONLY **ONE** WAY TO SETTLE THIS...

GRRRMPH...
SO SOFT, I DON'T NEED A PILLOW!
End

BATH TIME

STORMY NIGHT

CHECKERS

OKAY, SO THOSE ARE THE BASIC RULES. YOU'RE SURE YOU HAVE NEVER PLAYED BEFORE?

WHAT ARE YOU TWO UP TO?
I'M TEACHING ABU TO PLAY CHECKERS.

YOU'RE TEACHING *HIM?* AH, OKAY.

I HAVE A FEELING HE'LL BE A FAST LEARNER. I WOULDN'T PUT ANY MONEY ON IT, THOUGH.

REMEMBER, YOU CAN ONLY MOVE ONE SPACE DIAGONALLY. NOW YOU GO.

NO! IT HAS TO STAY ON THE TABLE!

NO, JUST LEAVE IT TO THE SIDE. WE'LL CHALK IT UP TO "BEGINNER'S YUCK."

THIS IS CALLED A "JUMP." IF YOU CAN GO OVER AN OPPONENT'S PIECE TO AN EMPTY SPACE, YOU CAN LAND ON THAT EXTRA SPACE...

...AND THEN YOU CAN TAKE THEIR PIECE OFF THE BOARD!

LET ME CLARIFY...

EEP!!!
WHAT IS IT?

CLUNK
AH, I SEE. IT WAS A DISTRACTION.

YOU AREN'T ALLOWED TO TAKE PIECES. THAT'S CHEATING! NOW PICK IT UP.

EVERYTHING YOU ARE DOING NOW IS ALSO CHEATING. EVERYTHING.

YOU LEFT A CORNER OPEN, SO THIS PIECE IS MINE. YOUR MOVE.

THAT'S DEFINITELY A MOVE I'VE NEVER SEEN BEFORE.

SO HOW ARE THE LESSONS COMING ALONG?

?
WELL, HE PULLED THE BAGHDAD BEETLE FLIP, THE SAND SWITCHEROO, A MIDNIGHT DOUBLE CLOUD, AND A NEW VARIATION ON THE SCARAB SHUFFLE.

OH, YOU THOUGHT I WAS FALLING FOR THOSE EASY SCAMS? I WAS LEARNING YOUR OTHER TRICKS. AND YOUR SLEIGHT OF HAND IS GETTING A LITTLE LAZY, LATELY.

SHE LIKES TO KEEP HER STRATEGY ONE JUMP AHEAD TOO.

End

POCAHONTAS

MOOD WIND

wshhhssshhhh

WWWWWWWHHSSSSHHHHH

THE WIND DOESN'T FEEL LIKE TALKING TODAY.
End

AN APPLE A DAY

VERY WELL, MEEKO.

I THINK YOU'VE BURNED OFF ENOUGH ENERGY TO HAVE THAT SNACK NOW.
End

HURRY BACK

I'M SO LATE FOR THE FESTIVAL!
NOT TO WORRY.

I TAUGHT MEEKO HOW TO BRAID QUICKLY.

THANK YOU! I MUST HURRY BA--

THE DREAM ROUTINE

QUE QUE NA-TO-RA..

...YOU WILL UNDERSTAND...
GOOD DAY, CHILD.
GRANDMOTHER WILLOW, I CAME TO TELL YOU ABOUT A DREAM I HAD LAST NIGHT.

OOOH, A **DREAM!** I DO LIKE A GOOD DREAM!
I KNOW YOU DO.

WAIT, IS THIS THE ONE WHERE PEOPLE GROW LEAVES ON THEIR ARMS?
NO...
OH, PITY. I LIKE THAT ONE.

IN MY DREAM, I WAS SITTING ON A HILL...

I LOOKED UP AT THE SKY AND SAW TWO CLOUDS.
ONE CLOUD WAS SHAPED LIKE A HILL. THE OTHER WAS SHAPED LIKE ME, SITTING.

AND THAT'S NOT EVEN THE MOST INTERESTING PART!
MY FRONDS TREMBLE IN ANTICIPATION, DEAR...
?

MEEKO WAS IN MY DREAM!

WE JUST... **STARED** AT ONE ANOTHER FOR A MINUTE OR SO.

AND THEN, HE DECIDED TO LEAVE. SO...HE LEFT!
?!

AND THAT'S NOT EVEN THE MOST INTERESTING PART!
I AM **GREATLY** ANTICIPATING THE "INTERESTING PART," DEAR.

IN THIS DREAM, I WAS APPROACHED BY A MIGHTY STAG!
AH, **NOW** IT'S GETTING INTERESTING...

IT BECKONED ME TO SPEAK WITH HIM.
FASCINATING!

UNDER GLINTS OF MOONLIGHT, THE STAG STOOD PROUD AND TOLD ME THESE WORDS...
WHAT DID HE SAY, CHILD? **WHAT DID HE SAY?**

HE ASKED ME FOR TURN-BY-TURN DIRECTIONS TO THE NEAREST RIVER! SO I DREW HIM A LITTLE MAP...
I THINK THIS **DREAM** IS GOING TO PUT ME TO **SLEEP.**

THEN, IN MY DREAM, I TURNED INTO A PINECONE.

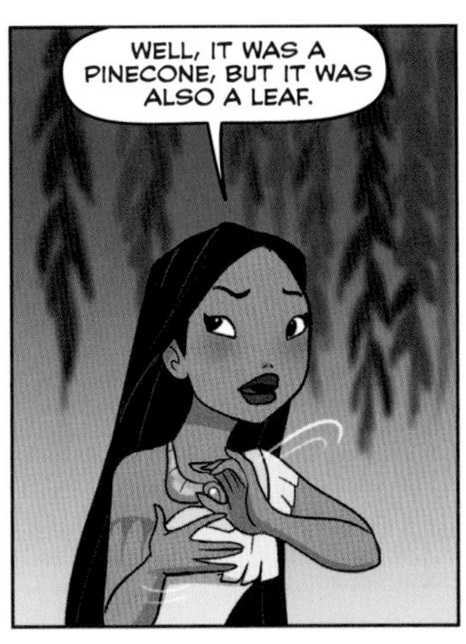
WELL, IT WAS A PINECONE, BUT IT WAS ALSO A LEAF.

I HAD THE THIN STEM OF A LEAF, BUT THE SCALES OF A PINECONE.

DOES THAT MAKE SENSE?
IT MAKES ME WONDER WHAT YOU ATE FOR DINNER LAST NIGHT, CHILD...

WHAT **DO** YOU THINK MY DREAM MEANT, GRANDMOTHER WILLOW?

THE DREAM MEANT...UH, **EAT WELL, SLEEP WELL, AND BE WELL!**

BUT GRANDMOTHER, YOU SAID THAT ABOUT THE **LAST** DREAM I TOLD YOU!

IT WORKED, DIDN'T IT?
MAYBE I'LL ASK KEKATA NEXT TIME...

NOT A WORRY

INCENTIVES

TRADITIONS

THE PEOPLE OF JAMESTOWN HAVE BEEN SHOWING ME THEIR WINTER CELEBRATIONS. THEY'RE VERY INTERESTING.

HOW SO?
WE TELL STORIES AND SHARE OUR DREAMS ON THE WINTER SOLSTICE, BUT THEY HAVE DANCES AND DECORATE THEIR HOMES!

YOU HUMANS, SO ODD. WE TREES JUST DROP OUR LEAVES AND GO TO SLEEP.

NOT VERY EXCITING, THOUGH!
WHEN YOU'RE 200 YEARS OLD, A GOOD NAP IS ***VERY*** EXCITING.

THEY PLACE THESE EVERGREENS ALL AROUND THEIR WINDOWS AND DOORS, UPON THEIR MANTLES, EVERYWHERE THEY CAN!

THEY HANG THESE POISON BERRIES UP HIGH FOR SAFETY, BUT FOR SOME REASON THEY EXPRESS ***AFFECTION*** BENEATH THEM!

≶HMPH≷ I SUPPOSE IT WON'T BE LONG UNTIL THEY JUST DECORATE THE TREES THEMSELVES!

NONSENSE, TREES ARE BEAUTIFUL THE WAY THEY ARE.

I KNOW YOU CAN'T EAT THEM, BUT I WANTED TO SHOW YOU SOME OF THE CAKES AND TREATS THEY MAKE!

SUPPLIES ARE SCARCE, BUT THEY HAVE COMBINED CLOVES, BUTTER, RAISINS, AND-- ***OH NO!!!***

WHERE ARE THEY?!?

ASK YOUR FURRY BOTTOMLESS PIT, CHILD, HE'S HEAVIER THAN USUAL.
End

ROCK DRAWINGS

FORK IN THE RIVER

HIDE AND SEEK

LET'S SEE, POCAHONTAS USUALLY HIDES IN THE TREES...*HM,* NOT THERE...

BRRZZZZ

OH, IT'S ONLY YOU, FLIT. WELL, KEEP DRINKING, POCAHONTAS COULD BE ANYWH--

WAAAAAAIT A MINUTE...
NOBODY HERE BUT US LUPINES!
!

POCAHONTAAAASSS... COME ON, CAN I GET A ***HINT,*** AT LEAST?!

I WANTED TO GO VISIT THE CAVES. AT LEAST IT'S COOL IN THERE!

THAT'S IT! I'M TIRED AND HOT AND I'M GOING IN HERE FOR A REST. NO MORE HIDE AND SEEK!

SERIOUSLY?
DON'T PEOPLE GIVE UP **SO** QUICKLY?

ALL RIGHT, OH CHAMPION OF HIDE AND SEEK, LET'S HEAR YOUR HIDING WISDOM!
YOU HAVE TO THINK LIKE THE ANIMALS!

HOW DOES THE LIZARD HIDE FROM THE EAGLE? HE BECOMES ONE WITH THE ROCK! THE BOBCAT HIDES IN THE DAPPLED SHADOWS!

IN A TREE, FLIT BECOMES NOTHING BUT A TINY LEAF.
WHAT ABOUT RACCOONS?

FOOD HIDES IN ***THEM.***

End

LAUGHING WARRIOR

KEKATA IS GOING TO ANOINT THE WARRIORS TONIGHT IN A SECRET CEREMONY!
I KNOW. FATHER WANTS ME TO GO, TO DRAW THE CORN CIRCLES.

YOU ARE SO LUCKY!
IT'S JUST TO ASK AHONE TO SOOTHE THE HEARTS OF THE WARRIORS AFTER THE BATTLE.

BUT AFTER THAT, THE MEN WILL DANCE AND THERE'LL BE THE FEAST...
YOU'RE RIGHT, I GUESS IT WON'T BE TOO BAD.

...AND YOU'LL SIT NEXT TO KOCOUM. SIIGH
OH. I'M SO EXCITED.

OH. HELLO, KOCOUM.
WINGAPO, POCAHONTAS.

...SO. READY FOR A WELL-DESERVED PARTY?
I LOOK FORWARD TO SLEEPING WITHOUT THE CALL OF THE DRUMS.

OH COME NOW...YOU CAN AFFORD TO, UM...CUT LOOSE A BIT! YOU'VE EARNED IT.
"CUT LOOSE"?

I'M WEARING MY WOLFS-EYE AMULET, IS THAT NOT ENOUGH?
THIS'LL BE A LONG NIGHT...

AHONE SMILES UPON YOU ALL AND BIDS YOU PEACE. NOW LET US REJOICE IN OUR VICTORY!

SO HELP ME, MR. SERIOUS, I WILL GET YOU TO LAUGH TONIGHT!

KOCOUM, WANT TO SEE SOMETHING FUNNY?

WHAT ARE YOU DOING?
EMBARRASSING MYSELF, APPARENTLY...

MY, KOCOUM, WHAT A MAGNIFICENT BUCKSKIN CAPE!
THANK YOU. I WON IT IN BATTLE.

WHAT A COINCIDENCE! I WAS IN A BATTLE ONCE AND GOT A FINE HAT FOR IT! LET ME SHOW YOU!

BOO!

THE BATTLE FOR THE LEFTOVERS, I ASSUME?
OKAY, SO I LOST...

KOCOUM, I CREATED A SPECIAL DANCE JUST FOR YOU, NOW WATCH!

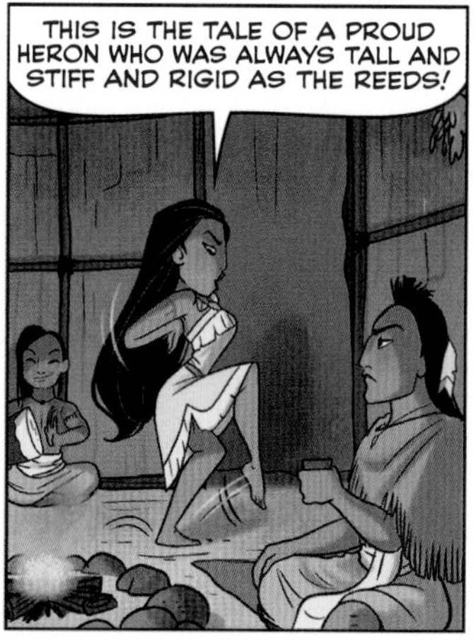
THIS IS THE TALE OF A PROUD HERON WHO WAS ALWAYS TALL AND STIFF AND RIGID AS THE REEDS!

ONE DAAAY.. THE **WIND** CAME TO VISIT! SHE BLEW ALL THROUGH HIS LONG SLICK FEATHERS....

...AND **TICKLED HIM!**
I AM NOT ITCHY, BUT I DO NEED A NEW DRINK.

I DON'T UNDERSTAND. HOW CAN SOMEONE NEVER EVER LAUGH?

HE **IS** A GREAT WARRIOR, THOUGH. HE HAS THE RESPECT AND ADMIRATION OF THE WHOLE TRIBE.

HRMMPPPHH... HAHAHAHAHAHA!

MEEKO, KOCOUM IS NOW THE LAUGHING WARRIOR.
BUT THAT'S OUR LITTLE SECRET!
End

Mulan

MEDITATION TRAINING

BOYS, I'VE BEEN THINKING WE MIGHT BE GETTING A BIT SOFT...
SOFT?!

WE HAVE ENJOYED THE SPOILS OF VICTORY. PEACE, HOME-COOKED MEALS, A COMFORTABLE PLACE TO REST.
MM, I GUESS...

IF EXPERIENCE HAS TAUGHT US ANYTHING, IT'S THAT WE NEED TO STAY SHARP, FOCUSED AND STRONG!
BUT A NAP AFTER A MEAL IS HOW I MEDITATE!

MEDITATION! THAT'S A GOOD START!
OR WE COULD BUILD A WALL TO DEFEND US. NOT A GREAT ONE, BUT DECENT.

TODAY WE WILL PRACTICE MEDITATION.

THE FIRST THING YOU MUST DO IS CLEAR YOUR HEAD OF ALL DISTRACTIONS.

GO INSIDE YOUR HEAD TO A CALMING MEMORY.
SOMEPLACE TRANQUIL, WHERE YOUR ENERGY CAN FLOW.
WHERE YOU CAN ESCAPE THE NOISE OF LIFE.
WHERE YOU CAN BE TRUE TO YOURSELF.
YOU WERE EXPECTING A TRANQUIL MEADOW?

OH, THEY'RE LEARNING CONCENTRATION! FOCUS.. SHEDDIN' DISTRACTIONS!

LET'S BUMP IT TO THE NEXT LEVEL!

MUSHU! MEDITATION ISN'T A CONTEST!

EXCUSE ME! WHEN CANNONS ARE GOING OFF ALL OVER AND YOU CAN FIND INNER PEACE...

...MAYBE YOU'LL REMEMBER WHO MADE YOU GONG STRONG!
DONK DONK DONK

HE HAS A POINT.
SEE? NOW LET'S GET MEDITATING. THIS IS HEAVY!

OKAY, LET'S GIVE THIS PEACE OF MIND A WHIRL.

AS I WAS SAYING, YOU MUST REMAIN QUIET IN ORDER TO FIND QUIET.
GOT IT!

THERE IS NO NEED TO RESPOND TO ANY EXTERNAL INFLUENCE.
ROGER THAT, 10-4! LOUD AND CLEAR!

BE QUIET!
SHOULD WE BE TAKING LESSONS FROM HER? SHE DOESN'T LOOK RELAXED AT ALL!

ONE MORE TIME. TRY TO RELAX.

BREATHE THROUGH YOUR NOSE, AND FIND YOUR RHYTHM.
snort

LET THE NOISE DRIFT AWAY. QUIET YOUR OWN THOUGHTS.

ARCHERY TRAINING

TODAY WE WILL BE REVISING OUR ARCHERY TECHNIQUE!

THE CENTER IS A DIRECT HIT. PERFECTION, THE IDEAL STRIKE.
YEAH, WE GRASP THAT MUCH, MULAN.

A NEAR HIT IS A NEAR MISS, AND WILL ONLY NEARLY DEAL THE DAMAGE INTENDED.

ANYTHING THIS FAR MEANS YOU'VE GIVEN YOUR ENEMY A FREE ARROW.
IF I PUNCH HIM, I CAN GET IT BACK!

BEFORE YOU CAN FIRE, YOU MUST DRAW YOUR BOW.

YOU MUST REMAIN STEADY, CALM, AND FOCUSED.

TEN MINUTES LATER...
KEEP HOLDING WHILE YOU WAIT FOR A PERFECT SHOT.

WHAT IS SHE WAITING FOR? IS IT S'POSED TO RUN AWAY?!

TRICK SHOT TIME!

THIS ISN'T REALLY THE POINT OF TRAINING.
PHTOOM!

THREE FOR THREE!
TOK

I PREFER CLOSE COMBAT!

REMEMBER NOT TO AIM FOR THE TARGET, BUT PAST IT.

FACTORING IN WIND, MOVEMENT, AND STRENGTH MEANS YOUR SHOT WILL HAVE THE FORCE NEEDED WHEN IT GETS THERE.

ARE YOU GOING TO SHOOT?
I LOOKED PAST THE TARGET AND SAW AN ADORABLE FOX ON THE NEXT HILL.

ANY BATTLE THAT CAN BE FOUGHT FROM A HILL AWAY IS FOR ME!
THOK!

IT'S FUN TO FIRE AT BALES OF HAY, ISN'T IT?
PTOY!

NOW IMAGINE THAT BALE OF HAY CAN SHOOT BACK.

THEY'RE GETTING CLOSER!!! RUN!!!

DEFENSIVE TRAINING

IF SOMEBODY COMES AT YOU WITH A RANGE WEAPON, THEY WILL HAVE MOMENTUM.

USE IT AGAINST THEM.

AVOID THE ATTACK AND DISORIENT THEM.

AND THAT'S HOW TO EXIT A BATTLE GRACEFULLY.
HE'S LIKE AN ANGRY SWAN, SO NICE.

DEFENSE IS ESPECIALLY IMPORTANT IN ARMED COMBAT.

THE BIGGER YOU ARE, THE MORE STRIKE POINTS YOU HAVE.
TOK!

TOO MUCH ARMOR WILL SLOW YOU DOWN, SO YOU MUST MANEUVER.
TOK
TOK
TOK

YOU'RE SUPPOSED TO DEFEND YOURSELF.
YOU NEVER SAID HOW.

INTIMIDATION WILL SERVE YOU BY LOWERING YOUR ATTACKER'S CONFIDENCE. LOOK THEM IN THE EYES AND SPEAK FROM YOUR WARRIOR SOUL.

I WISH US AN HONORABLE BATTLE.

PREPARE TO JOIN YOUR ANCESTORS!

NOT THE FACE!

ARM WRESTLING

HE LOST SO MANY TIMES, SO QUICKLY.
HIS HANDS WERE SO SOFT.
WHAT KINDA **MAN** IS HE?

I CAN'T BELIEVE MY COVER IS GOING TO BE BLOWN BY SOMETHING AS IDIOTIC AS ARM WRESTLING!

NOT TO WORRY, MULAN. FOR YOU SEE, I AM AN ARM WRESTLING MASTER...
AND I WILL TRAIN YOU.

YOU'RE AN ARM WRESTLING MASTER? BUT YOUR ARMS ARE AS THIN AS CHOW MEIN NOODLES.
OH, COME ON! THEY'RE ***AT LEAST*** A LO MEIN.

OKAY, GIVE ME EVERYTHING YOU'VE GOT, MULAN. DON'T HOLD BACK!

WAIT, I WASN'T READY!

ALRIGHT, LET'S TRY IT AGAIN, ***WHEN I'M READY*** THIS TIME.
...AAAAAAND ***BEGIN!***

WAIT, THERE WAS SOMETHING IN MY EYE! THAT LAST ONE DOESN'T COUNT!

ARM WRESTLING IS ABOUT MORE THAN DUMB STRENGTH. IT'S ABOUT THE SOPHISTICATED USE OF ***PSYCHOLOGY.***

READY... SET...AND AWAY WE ***GO!***

YOU LOOK RIDICULOUS.
RIDICULOU-*THHH* **AND** VICTORIOU-*THHH!*

YOU'VE GOTTA USE EVERY TRICK AT YOUR DISPOSAL TO WIN A MATCH.

READY... SET...LET IT GO!

PING! ONE HUNDRED PUSHUPS, NOW!
YES CAPTAIN SHANG!

THAT'S NOT VERY SPORTING.
ARM WRESTLING ISN'T A SPORT, MULAN. IT'S WAR!

YOUR TRAINING IS ALMOST COMPLETE. YOU HAVE ONE MORE TECHNIQUE TO LEARN, WHICH IS SURE TO DISTRACT ANY OPPONENT.
BREATHING FIRE!

LIKE THIS!

COUGH

THAT MAY WORK BETTER ON SPICY NOODLES NIGHT.
I'LL GRAB YOU SOME SZECHUAN PEPPER.

THE NEXT DAY...
I'D LIKE TO TRY AGAIN.
WHAT ARE YOU? A GLUTTON FOR PUNISHMENT?
ONE LOOK AT PING MAKES ME FEEL WEAK IN THE ARMS.

READY... SET... GO!

WHAT ARE WE GOING TO DO WITH ALL THESE EXTRA DUMPLINGS?
EXTRA DUMPLINGS?

...WHERE?

RING IN THE NEW YEAR

NOBODY WANTS TO BE HONORED WITH BORING NAPKINS.
THE BEST PARTIES ARE MADE IN THE LITTLE DETAILS.

JUST THINK, AT EVERY TABLE WHEN EVERY PERSON SITS TO EAT, THEY WILL SEE THEIR OWN PERSONAL DRAGON!

OH! I GET IT! LIKE *THIS!*

IF ONLY WE CELEBRATED A YEAR OF THE SWAN!

MAYBE I COULD HOST THE WHOLE EVENT! GIVE A SPEECH ABOUT WHAT DRAGONS MEAN TO EVERYBODY?

WE HAVE ALL OF THAT COVERED ALREADY--HOW OUR CELEBRATIONS WARD OFF THE DRAGON "NIAN" EACH YEAR. JUST ENJOY THE PARTY.
WHY DOES NIAN ALWAYS GET THE ATTENTION?

WELL AT LEAST LET ME DO THE COUNTDOWN FOR THE BALL DROP.
BALL DROP?

YOU MEAN JIE CAI CENG? THE GODS DESCENDING WITH WEALTH AND PROSPERITY?
YOU KNOW, BEING ANACHRONISTIC CAN BE VERY ALIENATING.

HERE YOU GO! HORNS, CLACKERS, TAKE YOUR PICK!

AND REMEMBER NOT TO USE THEM UNTIL THE MOMENT COMES!

DOES EVERYONE HAVE A NOISEMAKER?

I'M READY TO ROLL!

HAPPY NEW YEAR!

OOOOOOH!

THAT WAS BEAUTIFUL.

SO WHEN DO I OPEN MY PRESENTS?
THOSE ARE FOR THE CHILDREN.
End

FIREWORKS

AH, NOTHING LIKE A NICE *PENJING* TO PASS THE DAY.

HELLO!

AND A GOOD DAY TO YOU!

TRUSTING A DRAGON WITH FIREWORKS IS LIKE TRUSTING A RIVER WITH A SUGAR CUBE.

WHERE DO YOU THINK YOU'RE GOING WITH THOSE?

WHY, THE LAUNCH SITE, OF COURSE!

AND WHAT DO YOU PLAN ON DOING WITH THEM?

LAUNCHING THEM! YOU HAVE SEEN FIREWORKS BEFORE, RIGHT?

THIS IS A LOT OF FIREWORKS! HAVE YOU THOUGHT AT ALL ABOUT SAFETY?

HAVE I THOUGHT ABOUT **SAFETY?**

SHE WANTS TO KNOW IF I'VE THOUGHT ABOUT SAFETY!

WHAT'S "SAFETY"?

THESE ARE HIGHLY EXPLOSIVE AND DANGEROUS!

JUST ONE OF THESE COULD BLOW UP A HOUSE, NOT TO MENTION **YOU!**

DON'T WORRY. I'VE GOT A PLAN!

AND I'VE GOT A **FUSE!**

HOW IS THAT FUSE SUPPOSED TO MAKE ME FEEL BETTER?

I LIGHT THIS, AND IT GIVES ME TIME TO RUN AWAY IF I NEED TO.

IT'S JUST THAT YOU HAVE SUCH A SHORT FUSE.

A **SHORT FUSE!** WHY I NEVER! I HAVE A PERFECTLY LONG AND NORMAL FUSE! WHY DOES EVERYONE THINK I'M GOING TO EXPLODE AT ANY MOMENT? IS IT BECAUSE I'M A DRAGON, AND I BREATHE **FIRE!** OF ALL THE RIDICULOUS...
siiiigh..

HAPPY? THE FIREWORKS ARE A FEW FEET FROM EACH OTHER, AND WE HAVE THIS SUPERLONG EXCESSIVE FUSE!

YES, NOW I'M ***VERY*** HAPPY!
End

MUSHU'S REVIEW

SO YOU SAY THE GHOSTS OF MY ANCESTORS WANT TO KNOW HOW YOU'RE DOING?

I DON'T SEE WHY I NEED AN ANNUAL REVIEW. MY WORK SPEAKS FOR ITSELF!

I'VE NOTICED, AND HAVE A SUGGESTION.

IF YOUR WORK CAN'T SAY ANYTHING NICE, MAYBE IT SHOULDN'T SAY ANYTHING AT ALL!

ARE YOU SURE THEY'RE HERE? IT LOOKS EMPTY.
MUSHU, YOU KNOW SHE CAN'T SEE US.

AHEM...YOUR ACCOMPLISHMENTS.

YOU CLEANED THE FOUNTAIN.
TWICE!

DO YOU HAVE ANY TASKS TO ADD TO THE LIST?

I'VE BEEN AN EAR TO CRY IN, AND A SHOULDER TO LISTEN!

THAT CAN'T BE RIGHT. MY EAR WOULD BE A LOT MORE DAMP...UH...

TALK TO MY LAWYER!
WHO AM I TALKING TO?

JUST TELL THEM SOMETHING NICE!
IT'S, AH, TRUE! MUSHU HAS BEEN A GREAT HELP AROUND THE VILLAGE!

WHY, THIS PAST WEEK ALONE, HE'S...

THERE WAS ONE TIME HE...UM...

THERE HASN'T BEEN A SINGLE ELEPHANT STAMPEDE SINCE HE'S BEEN OUR GUARDIAN!
IS THAT A THING?
SHHH!

NOW LET'S TAKE A LOOK AT DAMAGES AND INCIDENTS YOU'VE CAUSED, MUSHU.

NOW WHAT ARE THEY DOING?
GETTING OUT THE LIST OF COMPLAINTS.

NOTHING YOU CAN'T HANDLE, THOUGH.

HOW LONG IS THE LIST?
IT'S HARD TO TELL. IT STOPPED ROLLING AT THE PAGODA.

AND AS YOU CAN SEE HERE, THE AVALANCHE REDIRECTED THE RIVER, WHICH MADE IT CLOSER WHEN THE STABLE FIRE BROKE OUT.

THE FIRE YOU STARTED?

EXACTLY! THEY CANCEL EACH OTHER OUT!

IF I'M HEARING HIS SIDE CORRECTLY, WHO BETTER CAN PROTECT US FROM MUSHU, BUT MUSHU HIMSELF!

WHAT HAPPENS NOW?
SSH, THEY'RE MAKING THEIR DECISION.

IF I DON'T PASS THIS REVIEW, I'LL BE DEMOTED FROM GUARDIAN AND BACK TO RUBBING FA BAO'S BUNIONS AGAIN!

YEEEE-HAAAAAAA!!! I PASSED!!!!!
OH GOOD! NOW, ABOUT MY LAWYER'S FEE..
End

BENT OUTTA SHAPE

WELL, NOW I'VE SEEN EVERYTHING. MULAN'S TURNED HERSELF INTO A NOODLE!

STRETCHING KEEPS ME LIMBER, HELPS ME DO THIS!
PFFT! LIMBER? DRAGONS INVENTED LIMBER! WATCH...

PLEASE DON'T TELL THE ANCESTORS.
End

Tiana

BEIGNET STAND

NAVEEN, THIS BEIGNET STAND IS A GREAT IDEA FOR PROMOTING THE RESTAURANT!
MY IDEAS ARE OCCASIONALLY STILL **BRILLIANT**, YES?

IT'S GONNA BE A LOTTA WORK BUT IF IT'S **BOTH** OF US, THEN WE SHOULD GET THROUGH IT JUS'--
OIL

--FINE AN' WHERE D'YOU THINK YOU'RE GOING?
HA-HAAAAA...

FORGIVE ME, TIANA, BUT I FORGOT I PROMISED TO ACCOMPANY LOUIS'S SET TODAY!
BUT WHAT ABOUT THE BEIGNETS?!

VOILA, MY REPLACEMENT!
LOTTIE?!
IT'S LIKE PLAYIN' KITCHEN WHEN WE WERE BABIES!

YOU'VE NEVER MADE A BEIGNET IN YOUR LIFE!
OH PISH, HOW HARD COULD IT BE?

HOW 'BOUT YOU HANDLE THE **SALES**.
OOH **MONEY**, **THAT** AH KNOW!

ALL SET, LOTTIE! LET'S OPEN FOR BUSINESS!
MISS TIANA'S FINEST BEIGNETS, COME AN' GET 'EM!!

LATER...
THAT'S ODD, WHY DID THE ORDERS SUDDENLY STOP?

I SHOULD HAVE KNOWN.
THIS **NICE** GENTLEMAN ASKED ME HOW MY DAY WAS, I HAD TO FILL HIM IN! SO, AFTER BREAKFAST...

THANKS FOR HELPING OUT, LOTTIE. I COULDN'T HAVE DONE THIS WITHOUT YOU.
ANYTIME, TIA HONEY!

AW, YOU'RE TUCKERED OUT! YOU JUST SIT A SPELL, I'LL START CLEANIN' UP...
OKAY, JUST FOR A MINUTE.

I'LL JUST TOSS THESE SACKS IN THE BARROW HERE...
NO, DON'T *TOSS* THEM, THAT'S THE--
POOF
--SUGAR.
SUGAR

I GOT AN EMERGENCY DRESS REPAIR, MAMA.
LET'S TAKE A LOOK.

WHAT ON EARTH DID THAT CHILD DO?
WOULD YOU BELIEVE LOTTIE FORGOT A POT OF COLD OIL WOULD BE HEAVY? *SPLOOSH.*

CAN YOU SALVAGE IT?
DOES SHE LIKE SCARVES?

ONCE I TRIMMED IT WITH SOME FRENCH LACE, IT CAME OUT REAL LOVELY.

OH EUDORA, IT'S JUS' *GORGEOUS!* AFTER THE MESS I MADE, I DON'T DESERVE SUCH FRIENDS...!

I'LL KEEP IT FOREVER!
OH LOTTIE, DARLIN', NO NEED TO CRY!

UH-OH, THAT'S HER *EXTRA*-PERMANENT MASCARA!
SnooooOrt
DOES SHE LIKE HANDKERCHIEFS?
End

TRYOUTS

YOU WANT TO WHAT, LOTTIE?
IT'S THE MODERN WAY, TIANA! I INVITE ALL THE ELIGIBLE MEN TO CONVINCE ME WHY THEY'RE WORTHY OF MY ATTENTIONS!

SOUNDS LIKE WHEN YOU SHOP FOR SHOES!
YES! EXCEPT GENTLEMEN DON'T GIVE YOU BLISTERS!

WELL IF YOU'RE GONNA TRY THIS, YOU TRY IT HERE IN THE RESTAURANT, OKAY?
OH TIA, YOU'RE A PEACH, THANK YOU!!

ORDER EXTRA CLEAN TABLECLOTHS, LOTTIE THROWS DRINKS.
OH. I KNOW.

OH TIA, IT ALL LOOKS SIMPLY MAHVELOUS!

DON'T THANK ME YET. I'M GOING TO CHAPERONE EVERY ONE OF YOUR DATES.

AND JUST WHAT MAKES YOU THINK I CAN'T JUDGE FOR MYSELF?

I'M LEARNING CURSIVE, SO I CAN WRITE LOVE LETTERS NOW!

I THINK THE RAILROADS WILL PUT THIS TOWN ON THE MAP!

IT'S ALREADY ON THE MAP. IT HAS A NAME AND EVERYTHING.
SHH! HE'S INTERESTED IN BUSINESS!

I WOULD JUST NEED A SWEET INVESTMENT TO GET ME GOING.

THEIR FAMILY MAY BE SUGAR RICH, BUT YOU JUST SOURED YOUR CHANCES.

I'VE DONATED HEAVILY TO ORPHANAGES, BUT IT'S NEVER REALLY ENOUGH.
YOU HAVE OUR ATTENTION.

MAYBE YOU COULD GET THE **CHILDREN** SOME PUPPIES TO PLAY WITH AND RAISE?

UGH! PUPPIES? THEY SMELL, AND YIP, AND ROLL AROUND IN FILTH!

WHO DOESN'T LIKE ***PUPPIES?***
THANK YOU. NEXT?

SO TELL US A LITTLE BIT ABOUT YOURSELF.

WELL I WAS RAISED UP IN THE NORTHEAST, ATTENDED ONLY THE FINEST SCHOOLS, WHERE I WAS TRAINED IN FENCING AND HORSE RIDING. NOT AT SAME TIME, MIND YOU! WOULD BE TOO DANG

...AND WE WENT ON AN ADVENTURE TO THE CONGO, WHERE I LEARNED FOURTEEN LANGUAGES. I CAN ALSO PILOT SMALL AIRCRAFT, AND AM

AND I'M AN EXCELLENT LISTENER!
WAKE UP! I THINK HE'S WRAPPING UP!
Z

IT'S SO NICE TO SEE YOU AGAIN, LOTTIE!
AGAIN?

THIS IS TRAVIS.
TRAVIS?
YOU MET AT THE BALL. AND THEN THE PARADE.
AND MY GRAND OPENING.

????

WHAT A LOVELY...UM...
NAPKIN. YOU HAVE ONE, TOO.

LOUIS'S FAN CLUB

LUNGE/CRUNCH

SPICY ALLIGATOR

I'M A LITTLE NERVOUS, IF I'M BEING HONEST!

NONSENSE!
IF THEY DON'T LIKE YOU, THEN THEY DON'T KNOW JAZZ!

THAT'S WHAT I'M WORRIED ABOUT! WHAT IF THEY DON'T KNOW JAZZ, AND I'M WASTING MY TALENT ON THEM?

WELL **NOBODY** CAN HEAR YOU IN THE LITTLE GATOR'S ROOM!

LADIES AND GENTLEMEN, TONIGHT WE HAVE A FEAST FOR NOT JUST YOUR APPETITES, BUT YOUR EARS!

PLEASE GIVE A WARM WEL-COME TO THE BEST HORN IN THE BAYOU: **LOUIS!**

IT'S **SHOWTIME!**
THUD

NOW HANG ON A DANG MINUTE! DON'T START DANCING UNTIL I START PLAYIN'!

EVERYONE PLEASE CALM DOWN!
YOU HAVEN'T EVEN PAID YOUR TABS!

I KNOW HE'S AN ALLIGATOR, BUT HE'S AN AMAZING MUSICIAN TOO! HE'S MY **FRIEND!**

YOU PUT A SIGN UP TELLING THEM WHAT TO EXPECT, RIGHT?

OF COURSE!
Tiana's Palace
TONIGHT'S SPECIAL
SPICY GATOR!

SORRY FOR THE CONFUSION, FOLKS! I ASSURE YOU THE ONLY THING ON THE MENU FROM ME TONIGHT IS SOME TASTY JAMS!

THIS FIRST DELICIOUS LICK IS INSPIRED BY SOME FIREFLY I KNEW WHO HAD LOVE IN HIS HEART. GLOWED BRIGHTER THAN HIS TAIL SIDE!

LOUIS, THEY DON'T UNDERSTAND "GATOR" LIKE NAVEEN AND I DO.
NOW HUSH, MY ACCENT AIN'T ***THAT*** THICK!

BESIDES, BUG OR BARON, EVERYONE UNDERSTANDS ***LURVE IS LURVE*** WHEN THEY HEA' IT!
AMEN!

IT'S A LITTLE CHILLY OUT THERE, NO?

COME ON!

ASHIDANZA, BOUNCE THEM HOT NOTES, LOUIS!

THIS ALLIGATOR JAZZ REMINDS ME OF WHEN I WAS YOUNG!
EVERYONE IS YOUNG AGAIN ON A DANCE FLOOR!

Y'ALL ARE JUST TOO KIND! MWAH! MWAH!

THANK YOU FOR COMING OUT AND GIVING LOUIS A CHANCE!
THAT'S ONE GREAT GATOR!

AND THANK ***YOU!***
HA-***HA!*** NOW, ABOUT MAH COMPENSATION....

I ACCEPT CASH, CHECK, OR A BIG OL' PILE OF LEFTOVERS.
YOU'RE IN LUCK, IT'S ÉTOUFÉE NIGHT!
End

SOME LIKE IT HOTTER

A-HA! I KNEW THE GOOD STUFF WAS AROUND HERE SOMEWHERE.
THAT SAUCE IS WICKED, TIANA. WATCH YO'SELF!

TIANA SITS BACK DOWN FOR BRUNCH.
...AH WAS JUST APPALLED BY HOW LITTLE FAIRY JEWELRY THEY HAD...
ALL RIGHT, THIS SAUCE HAS GOTTA BE HOT ENOUGH.

REALLY? THIS ONE IS WEAKER'N A BABY KITTEN!

...AH WAS SO UPSET AT HIM, AH WAS PRACTICALLY FUMIN'...
OH, THIS KITTEN'S GOT CLAWS! THIS KITTEN'S GOT CLAWS!

...SO AH'M PRACTICING MAH WAVE FOR THE FLOAT, CAUSE YA GOTTA HAVE JUST THE RIGHT WAVE...
TOO HOT! TOO HOT!

...AND THIS HANDSOME MAN SEES ME WAVING ON THE BENCH IN THE PARK...

...AND SO AH SAY, "IF ONLY SOME TALL DRINK OF WATER COULD HELP ME DOWN FROM HERE"...

THIS IS NOT WORKING...
SPLOOSH

MY MOUTH IS BURNING!
HERE'S A SODA POP, MISS!

OH NO, SODA WILL MAKE IT WORSE!
LEMME TRY FANNING YOUR TONGUE.

'OWWW, I'S S'ILL BUR'ING!
THERE'S ONLY ONE WAY TO CURE THIS!

MORE HOT SAUCE! WE GOTTA COUNTERACT THE FIRST ONE!
HELP!

DOES ANYBODY HERE KNOW A CURE FOR HOT SAUCE BURNIN'?

FLOUR
I WILL NEVER TASTE ANYTHING AGAIN!

THIS IS RIDICULOUS, I NEED SOMETHING ELSE...

THERE!
MILK

glug
glug
glug

AAAAAHHH!
MILK

HOT SAUCE IS... THE BEE'S KNEES... AND MILK IS... THE BUG SPRAY.
MILK

...AND THAT'S HOW AH DECIDED TO FORGET THE GLOVES AND JUST MAKE MAH FINGERNAILS SPARKLE.

WHAT DO YA THINK, TIA? DOES MAH OUTFIT SOUND WONDERFUL?

YEAH, CHARLOTTE. I THINK IT'LL BE RED HOT.

OH GOODIE, GOODIE, GOODIE!
End

CHILI

MMMMM...SMELL THAT CUMIN? ONION, PEPPER, EVEN CINNAMON! ALL THE AROMAS OF A GREAT CHILI COOK-OFF!

AND TO THINK, I GET TO ***JUDGE*** IT THIS YEAR! THIS GIRL'S ***MOVING UP!***
CHILI COOKOF
WELCOME
JUDGE

IT WOULDN'T BE FAIR TO ALLOW YOU INTO THE COMPETITION AGAIN.
I'LL TAKE THAT AS A COMPLIMENT.
BAYOU BILL
JUDGE

IT WASN'T GIVEN AS ONE.
THAT'S WHY I HAD TO TAKE IT!
BIG JIM'S
JUDGE

TIANA! I SEE YOU'VE SAVED THE BEST FOR FIRST!
LA BOU SUG

I GREW UP ON YOUR SPICY SWEET CHILI! IT SET MY OPINION ON WHAT CHILI SHOULD BE!

THAT'S WHY I WANTED TO SURPRISE YOU! MORE PEPPERS, MORE BROWN SUGAR! MY CHILI HAS FINALLY GROWN UP TOO!

WATER, MILK, SWEET TEA, ASPIRIN, OR ICE PACK?

NAVEEN! WHAT ARE YOU DOING HERE?
AS YOUR HUMBLE HUSBAND, I KNOW I'M INELIGIBLE, IN EVERY SENSE.
TIANA'S PALACE
FREE SAMPLES
JUDGE

BUT THIS WAS THE ONLY WAY I COULD THINK OF TO GET YOU TO TRY ***MY*** COOKING FOR A CHANGE!
JUDGE

YOU JUST NEVER KNOW HOW THINGS ARE GOING TO GO TOGETHER, DO YOU?
PINEAPPLE AND LICORICE?

MY CHILI IS LIKE MY JAZZ-FREE FLOWING, OPEN TO INSPIRATION!
I JUST KEEP ADDING THINGS AS I GET THE HANKERING, FLAVOR ON FLAVOR!

I CAN SEE! ONIONS, TOMATO, PEPPERS, CABBAGE, CHICKEN...

OH, SURE! AND CRAWDAD, SNAIL, PEAT MOSS, EEL, PAPRIKA, PINCH OF SALT...

MAMA ODIE! IF YOUR CHILI IS AS MAGIC AS YOUR MAGIC, YOU'RE STIRRING UP A NICE SURPRISE!

NOW YOU DON'T KNOW HALF WHAT THIS HERE MAGIC GUMBO POT CAN DO!

A GOOD CHILI GOTTA CAST A MIGHTY SPELL ON YO' TASTE BUDS, ELSE WHY BOTHER?
I RECKON THAT'S WHY WE KEEP OUR RECIPES UNDER LOCK AND KEY.

FOR YOU, I CAN SHARE!

THERE WERE SO MANY GOOD CHILIS TODAY!

...AND FROM SO MANY OF MY CLOSE FRIENDS!
LA BOUFF
SUGAR

IN FACT, PICKING ONE OF THEM ALMOST WOULDN'T SEEM FAIR. SO THIS YEAR'S WINNER...

...IS TRAVIS!
HUH? MINE WAS JUST KETCHUP AND CELERY!
JUDGE
End

WORD OF MOUTH

WHAT DO YOU HAVE THAT'S NOT SEAFOOD?

HUSH PUPPIES! THAT'LL BE DIFFERENT!

BRUSSELS SPROUTS! BROCCOLI! BRUSSELS SPROUTS! BROCCOLI!

I'M TRYING TO BREAK SOME OLD HABITS, SO...
LET ME GUESS... WELL DONE, HEAVY ON THE GARLIC?
YES!

WHAT A BUSY DAY! IS THERE A PARADE OR A FESTIVAL YOU DIDN'T TELL ME ABOUT?

NOT THAT I KNOW ABOUT. MOST OF THESE FOLKS AREN'T REGULARS, SO IF I DIDN'T HEAR ABOUT IT, I DON'T KNOW HOW ***THEY*** WOULD'VE.
WHY DON'T WE JUST ASK THEM?

SO WHAT BRINGS YOU IN TODAY? THE FESTIVAL?
RANDOM CRAVING.
I'M NOT FOND OF PARADES.
I'M TIRED OF THE SAME GARBAGE EVERY DAY. TREAT YOURSELF!

TIANA! SIT DOWN! YOU'RE FRAZZLED, AREN'T YOU?
THE RESTAURANT WAS SWAMPED TODAY! I MEAN ***LITERAL*** SWAMP CREATURES.

YOU FINISHED THE SPELL, DIDN'T YOU?
YOU NEVER WANT TO LEAVE A SPELL UNFINISHED, IN CASE IT DECIDES TO FINISH ITSELF.

I JUST WANT TO DO THIS ***MY*** WAY. I WANT TO ***EARN*** MY SUCCESS.
YOU EARNED SOME GOOD FRIENDS. ***THAT'S*** SUCCESS.

BESIDES, MY MAGIC GOT THEM ***IN*** THE DOOR. YOUR MAGIC GONNA KEEP THEM ***COMING BACK!***
End

IN WITH THE NEW

BABA AU RHUM, SHRIMP MIRLITON, CREOLE TURTLE SOUP, ROAST DUCK...ANYTHING I'M FORGETTING?

THANKS FOR YOUR TIME TODAY, EVERYONE! Y'ALL GOT SERVINGS TO TAKE HOME FOR YOUR FAMILIES, RIGHT?
IT'S OUR PLEASURE, TIANA! HAVE A GOOD NIGHT!

AHHH! IT SMELLS SO WONDERFUL, MY NOSE REFUSES TO QUESTION YOUR METHODS. BUT I HAVE TO ASK....

AREN'T WE MISSING SOMETHING? LIIIKE... DINERS?

FOOD'S DONE, WE JUST HAVE TIME TO DECORATE. LADDER, NAVEEN.

IN MALDONIA, WE ALWAYS LEFT A LITTLE PLATE OF CAKES OUT FOR GRANDFATHER FROST!
IS THIS NORMAL IN AMERICA, TO MAKE SO MUCH FOOD?

IF YOU REMEMBERED TO COME TO OUR STAFF MEETINGS, YOU'D KNOW WHY, HONEY.

HEY LOTTIE! HOW WAS THE GARDEN DISTRICT?
OOH, IT'S NOT HOLIDAYS WITHOUT SEEING THOSE HOMES DECKED OUT!

SPEAKING OF DECKED OUT, DADDY WASN'T TOO KEEN ON PARTING WITH THOSE OLD SUITS O'HIS.
WELL IT IS FOR A GOOD CAUSE...

BUT THEN I REMINDED HIM IF HE WANTS THEM OLD THINGS TO FIT, HE CAN GIVE UP A FEW EXTRA COURSES AT RÉVEILLON TONIGHT! THAT DID IT!

THESE ARE THE ONES THAT ARE A LITTLE SNUG AROUND THE WAIST...

THAT'S LOUIS'S TRUMPET! THEY'RE HERE!

WELL LOOK AT YOU, "PAPA NOEL"!
THAT OR THE PIED PIPER! 'CEPT I'M ONLY LEADIN' FINE UPSTANDIN' FOLKS!

IMPRESSIVE COSTUME TOO!
PSHAW! THIS PAPA NOEL GOES BIG OR GOES HOME!

C'N I TAKE A REST, NOW? N'AWLINS IN DECEMBER IS STILL AWFUL MOIST!
FWOOSH!

WELCOME, COME IN! PLENTY FOR EVERYONE!
YOU CAN HAVE YOUR SOUP SPICY, OR VERY SPICY!

I HAVEN'T WORN A SUIT THIS NICE IN YEARS.
IT'S YOURS T'KEEP! THE HOLIDAYS ARE ABOUT SHARING WITH FAMILY, AREN'T THEY?

NEW ORLEANS HAS BEEN SO GOOD TO US, IT'S OUR TURN TO GIVE BACK.

TODAY, ALL OF NEW ORLEANS IS FAMILY TO US!
I NOTICED. IS THAT A GATOR IN A FAKE BEARD BY THE PUNCH BOWL?
End

MARDI GRAS

SAY, WHERE'S THAT JUJU O' YOURS? YOU DON'T GO NOWHERE WITHOUT THAT SNAKE!

OH JUJU JUST FINE, HE'S JUS' DOIN' MARDI GRAS HIS WAY...
LOOK FOR YOURSELF LOUIS.

End

Rapunzel

RAPUNZEL'S ONE WOMAN (AND PET) SHOW

Act 3
"The Pied Ponytail"

THE PIED PONYTAIL PLAYED A MAGIC MELODY TO LEAD ALL THE RATS OUT OF THE KINGDOM.

I SAID, "**ALL** THE RATS." WE'RE MISSING ONE ***VERY IMPORTANT*** RAT!

AWWW, COME ON, PASCAL. YOU ***PROMISED!***
TPHT!

Act 4
"The Princess & the Pea-scal!"

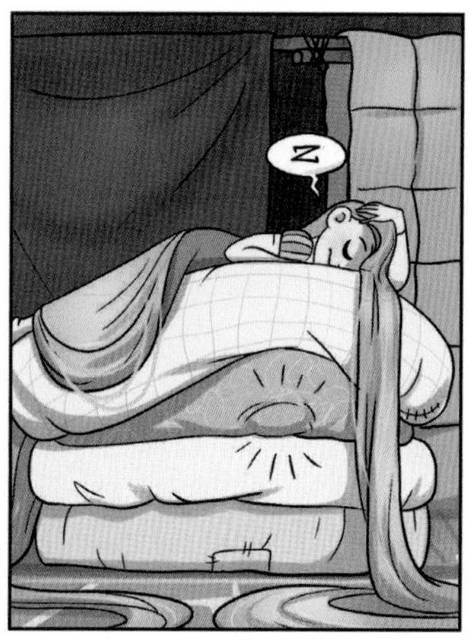
Z

Z
STOP IT, MOTHER, I ALREADY BRUSHED MY HAIR TODAY...
Z

CURSES, YOU HAVE VANQUISHED ME, SIR BEEFCAKE! I SHALL HAVE MY REVENGE YET!

IF YOU DARE RETURN, LORD CREEPYFACE, YOU'LL REGRET SQUANDERING MY GENEROUS MERCY! ***BEGONE!***

THEN SIR BEEFCAKE AND THE FAIR LADY PRETTYPUFF LIVED HAPPILY EVER AFTER!!
TA-DAAAAH!!!

WOW, TOUGH CROWD TONIGHT.
PFFT!

End

DON'T BLINK

HIDE AND SEEK

DRY TIME

THWOSH

NOTHING LIKE A NICE, WINDY DAY OUTSIDE TO DRY MY HAIR A LITTLE FASTER.

???

!!!

?

NO, NO, NO, NO! OW!

I SAID, "CAN YOU PLEASE UNTIE MY HAIR WHILE YOU'RE OVER THERE?"

WHAT? FOOD? SURE, YOU CAN HAVE A TREAT AFTER YOU UNTIE MY HAIR!

NO! WHERE ARE YOU GOING? CUT IT OUT!

COME BACK HERE!!!

GREAT. NOW WHAT?

KRA-KOW

SPLAPP

SPLASH
SLUSH

I'M SORRY, BUT YOU ALREADY ATE EVERYTHING!

YOU HAD YOUR CHANCE. NOW YOU HAVE TO WAIT FOR THIS TO DRY TO GET BACK DOWN.

THEN I DISCARD?
CHT! CHT!
I'M SORRY, I ONLY EVER LEARNED SOLITAIRE.
End

DRYING DAY

WASH DAY...
HOUR THREE OF DRYING...
...THE CHAMELEON STILL FAILS TO BRING ME SNACKS.
End

RAPUNZEL

AHOY MATEYS

SHADOW PUPPETS

LAVA

YOU KNOW THE RULES PASCAL...

...FIRST ONE TO TOUCH THE HOT LAVA LOSES!

I DON'T CONSIDER THIS CHEATING, DO YOU?

THREE DAYS LATER.
OBVIOUSLY, IT'S A TIE.
End

WORD OF THE DAY

GUESS WHAT TIME IT IS, PASCAL? THAT'S RIGHT, IT'S **WORD OF THE DAY** TIME.
BOTANY

AND TODAY'S WORD IS... *CONCOLOROUS:* UNIFORMLY COLORED, OR COLORED THE SAME THROUGHOUT...
BOTANY

CON-*COLOR*-OUS! ***GREAT*** WORD. SO LYRICAL! THE CHALLENGE IS TO FIND A WAY TO USE THE WORD TODAY.

I'VE GOT IT, PASCAL. WE'RE GOING TO CALL THIS MURAL, ***THE OPPOSITE OF CONCOLOROUS.***
I THINK IT STILL COUNTS?
End

BIRD'S-EYE VIEW

THAT ONE LOOKS LIKE A RABBIT WITH THREE EARS... AND THAT ONE LOOKS LIKE AN UPSIDE-DOWN... QUESTION MARK... *YAWN*

THE LAST TIME THIS HAPPENED I WASTED MY CHANCE, BUT STAY... RIGHT... THERE.

JUST SIT STILL A LITTLE LONGER, PLEASE. I REALLY APPRECIATE THE BIRD'S-EYE VIEW!
End

PASCART

ERGH, WE'RE OUT OF THE BLUE PAINT AGAIN, PASCAL.

MODERN ART! I LOVE IT. NOW HOW LONG CAN YOU HOLD THAT POSE?
End

RAINY DAY

TIME TO RISE AND SHINE, PASCAL! IT'S A NEW DAY!
FLING

TIME TO LET SOME LIGHT IN!

KRA-KOOM

...THIRTY MILLION VOLTS OF IT!

PHEW, WELL **THIS** IS GOING TO TAKE A LITTLE MORE THAN THE USUAL MOP AND SHINE-UP!

I MEAN, THAT'S THE SNEAKIEST DOWNPOUR I'VE EVER SEEN! I ONLY HAD THE WINDOW OPEN FOR A SECOND!

ONLY ONE THING FOR THIS, PASCAL!

TIME FOR THE ***EMERGENCY*** MOP!

PHEW, ALL DONE AND IT'S ONLY 7:20!

OH NO. NO NO NO, THE CEILING'S ***LEAKING*** NOW?
DWOOP

QUICK, QUICK, NEED SOMETHING TO CATCH IT IN....

COOKING FOR ONLY TWO PEOPLE, WE WORK WITH WHAT WE'VE GOT!

THIS IS THE WORST STORM WE'VE HAD IN AGES, PASCAL. IT'S GETTING SO DARK IN HERE.

EXCELLENT IDEA! TIME TO MAKE OUR **OWN** LIGHT!

THAT'S MUCH BETTER. I'M GLAD I SAVED THESE FOR A RAINY DAY!

OH, COME ON!

I KNOW IT'S NOT PRACTICAL, BUT WE HAVE TO STOP THESE LEAKS **SOMEHOW!**

WHAT IF THIS RAIN **NEVER** STOPS, PASCAL? I'LL HAVE TO SIT HERE FOREVER LIKE A BAT AND EAT **BUGS** TO SURVIVE!

I WONDER IF THIS WORKS ON WOOD? "FLOWER, GLEAM AND GLOW..."

GASP
THAT'S CLOSE ENOUGH!
End

BAKING DAY

OOOH, THE MUFFINS ARE DONE.

AWW, I DIDN'T THINK THIS RECIPE WOULD MAKE SO **MANY!**

MOTHER AND I CAN'T POSSIBLY EAT THEM **ALL** BY **OURSELVES.**
SUCH A WASTE.

End

WORKOUT

HAIRMONY

HOW TO SLEEP

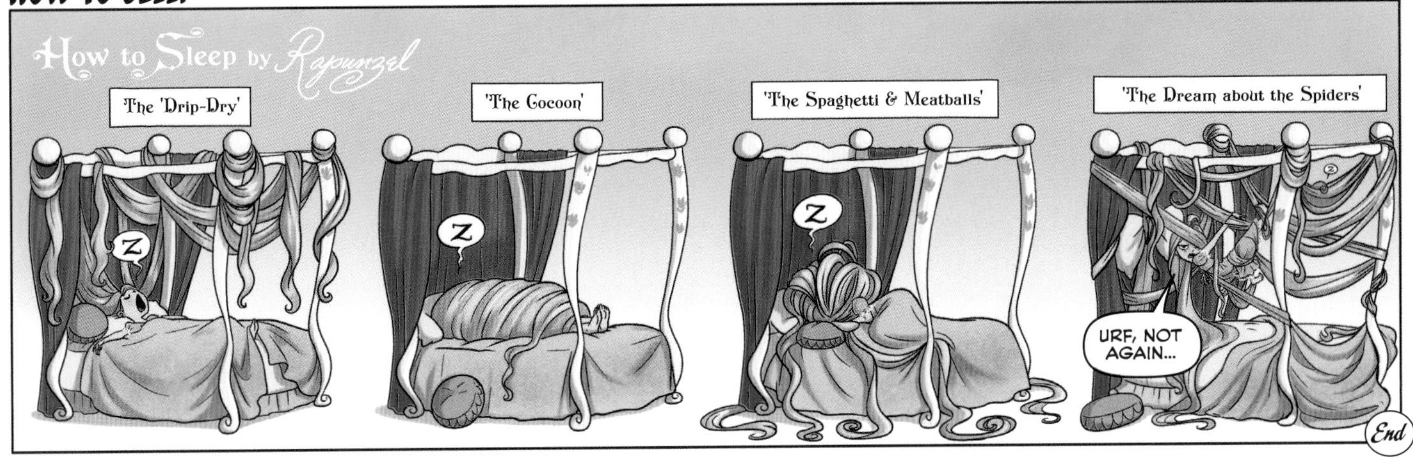

ROCK TALK

WAKE UP CALL

NICKNAMES

THE SMOULDER

RAP-STALLION

TAG, YOU'RE IT!

SORRY I'M LATE. I'M STILL TAKING THAT WRONG TURN AT THE THRONE ROOM.
I COULD GIVE YOU SOME TIPS. I CASED THE PLACE FOR WEEKS TO STEAL YOUR CROWN.

I COULD GET ANYWHERE IN THIS CASTLE WITH MY EYES CLOSED.
OH, THIS I *HAVE* TO SEE!

TAG! YOU'RE IT!!

YOU CAN TAKE OFF THE BLINDFOLD, EUGENE.

ARE YOU SURE YOU WANT TO GIVE UP YOUR ONE ADVANTAGE?

YOU FORGET--I'M USED TO LIVING HIGH ABOVE GROUND.
YOU...COULD HAVE JUST SAID...NO TAGBACKS!

munch munch munch munch
THIS GAME OF TAG IS ABOUT TO TAKE A TURN FOR THE--

WHAM!
WHUMP!

MUNCH MUNCH MUNCH MUNCH MUNCH
SO...MAYBE I'LL JUST GO FIND SOMEONE ELSE TO TAG?

GOT TO REMEMBER EUGENE IS TRICKY.

HAH. NICE TRY, EUGENE!

THANKS, I THOUGHT SO.
YOU'RE IT.
!

I SHOULD HAVE NOTICED--THE NOSE IS ALL WRONG!
hee hee hee!
WANTED

I THOUGHT MY SMOLDER GAVE ME AN UNFAIR ADVANTAGE IN LIFE, BUT I HAVEN'T SEEN PASCAL THE WHOLE TIME WE'VE BEEN PLAYING TAG.
AW, POOR PUMPKIN...
ARIANA REGINA

!

!!

YOU'RE IT!
TOTALLY WORTH IT.
End

EUGENE, LET DOWN YOUR HAIR

WHAT WE NEED IS A GUINEA PIG.

OH, I'VE DONE PIGS TOO. BIG PIGS **AND** SMALL PIGS.

DO PIGS EVEN HAVE THAT MUCH HAIR?

NOT WHEN I WAS DONE WITH THEM, THEY DIDN'T!

I THINK WE NEED TO FIND SOMEONE TO TEST YOUR BARBER SKILLS ON.

PERHAPS SOMEONE WITH FREE TIME ON HIS HANDS.

JUST A LITTLE OFF THE TOP.

LATER...
I'M PROUD OF YOU. AND YOUR HAIR LOOKS GREAT.

SHORTY DID A GREAT JOB. I CAN'T BELIEVE HOW NERVOUS I WAS. THANK GOODNESS YOU'RE SO BRAVE, YOU DIDN'T SEEM WORRIED AT ALL.

NO, NOT WORRIED AT ALL.
End

STREET ART

LOVELY DAY, ISN'T IT?
IT IS, PRINCESS, BUT I HEAR THEY'RE CALLING FOR RAIN LATER.

WELL, IT'S NOT RAINING YET! WE CAN EITHER SIT AROUND AND WAIT, OR ENJOY THE SUNSHINE!

WHAT ARE YOU DOING, PRINCESS?
DECORATING THE TOWN SQUARE.

YOU MIGHT NEED MORE CHALK.

WHY ARE THE ANTS ALL DIFFERENT COLORS?
WHAT ANTS?

THOSE ANTS.

OH, THOSE AREN'T ANTS. IT WILL ALL MAKE SENSE SOON. GOOD THINGS COME TO THOSE WHO WAIT!
WHAT IF I DON'T WANT TO WAIT?

PATIENCE IS A VIRTUE. TRUST ME ON--WHERE'D SHE GO?
THERE WAS A BUTTERFLY.

EXCUSE ME, PRINCESS, THOSE STARS ARE YELLOW.
THOSE AREN'T STARS.

THOSE STARS ARE BLUE.
THOSE AREN'T STARS, EITHER.

AT NIGHT THEY ALL MATCH. THESE DON'T MATCH.
THANK YOU FOR NOTICING.

YOU SHOULD GET THE SAME COLOR CHALK. IS THAT ORION?
SIGH HOW DID YOU GUESS?

YOU MIGHT WANT TO GET INSIDE, AND TRY AGAIN TOMORROW, PRINCESS.

I'VE SPENT TOO MANY DAYS WAITING FOR TOMORROW.

EVERYONE! FOLLOW ME!

THIS INN HAS A COVERED BALCONY!

SOMETIMES YOU CAN SIT AROUND AND WAIT, AND MAKE THE MOST OF THE DAY.
End

DUCKLINGS

WHAT DID YOU **DO** TO IT?!
IF YOU WANTED **DUCKLINGS** ON IT, YOU SHOULD HAVE SAID.
End

GLEAM AND GROW

HAPPY BIRTHDAY PASCAL! WHAT SHOULD WE DO FIRST, OPEN YOUR PRESENT OR--OH, OKAY, WE CAN MEASURE YOU.

YOU'VE UM, YOU'VE GROWN ABOUT A QUARTER OF AN INCH!

OH, IT'S NOT SO BAD, WE CAN'T ALL EXPECT TO GROW FOUR FEET A YEAR!
End

APPLE PIE

CAN YOU HAND ME ANOTHER APPLE?
OH, SURE!

MAAAAAX...
WHY IS A HORSE EVEN *IN* THE KITCHEN?

CAPTAIN OF THE GUARD, REMEMBER?
GUARDING AGAINST WHAT, MILDEW?
End

COUNTING STARS

I COUNT ONE THOUSAND, SIX HUNDRED AND TWENTY-TWO. I THINK THAT'S TWO MORE THAN YESTERDAY!
End

Merida

ARCHERY ASSIST

HAPPY ANNIVERSARY, ELINOR!
HOW **ROMANTIC,** FERGUS!

YOU REALLY **CAN** DO ANYTHING WITH YOUR ARROWS, CAN'T YOU?
WHAT DID YOU HAVE IN MIND?

HERE. IS **THIS** THE SPOT?

THUP
THUP
THUP
THUP

WELL, BOYS? DO YOU LIKE IT?
THUP
THUP
THUP

I'LL TAKE THAT AS A "YES."

OKAY, WEE ONES. LIGHTS OUT!
BOING
BABOING

LET ME GIVE YOU A HAND, MAUDIE!

SFOOK
WHOOOOOOSHHHH

SEE? LIKE I SAID, "LIGHTS OUT"!

OCH! THERE YOU ARE, MERIDA! I'M HOPING YOU CAN HELP ME WITH--

--MERIDA? SOMETHING WRONG?

OH DEAR.
Z Z Z Z

MERIDA LOVES HELPING US WITH HER ARCHERY SKILLS, BUT WE'VE BEEN RELYING ON HER SKILLS SO OFTEN...
...SHE HASN'T HAD TIME TO **SLEEP**
AYE, BUT HOW CAN WE MAKE THINGS RIGHT?
LEAVE THAT TO ME.

MERIDA!!!

BEHOLD! A HAMMOCK WORTHY OF SOMEONE WITH YOUR PARTICULAR GIFTS!

I WONDER IF SHE LIKES IT.
I THINK IT'S SAFE TO ASSUME SHE **DOES**.
End

SNEAKING

SLAP
SLAP
SLAP
SLAP

NOT SO LOUD, MERIDA! A LADY MOVES QUIETLY ABOUT THE CASTLE.

LATER...

I THOUGHT IT WAS A WEE BIT **TOO** QUIET...
End

CRAZY RIDE

SHOO NOW, YE WEE HORSE LICE!

OKAY, IF YE WANT TO GO FOR A RIDE, WE'LL GO FOR A RIDE **TOGETHER!**

SWOOSH
HOLD ON TIGHT!

EVERYTHING OKAY BACK THERE, BOYS?!?

THAT WAS THE SOFTEST LANDING **EVER,** ANGUS!

SO...WHERE ARE WE GOIN' NEXT?
THUD

COME BACK! THE **FUN** HAS JUST BEGUN!

MAYBE THEY'LL STICK TO HORSEY RIDES WITH **DAD** FROM NOW ON!
End

THEY COME IN THREES

JOIN THE FLOCK

STOLEN PIE

BABYSITTING

HOW ARE THEY CAUSING SUCH A MESS?

MAY AS WELL CLEAN WHILE I CAN NOW, LESS FOR LATER.

?!!

MAY AS WELL SAVE IT ALL FOR LATER.
TOK!

YOU WANT SUGAR, BOYS? HOW ABOUT SOME OF "MERIDA'S FAMOUS JINGLING TARTS"?

HALLOO! WHO CAN CATCH THESE WEE RUNAWAY PASTRIES?
ding
ding
ding

THIS'LL WEAR YOU OUT!

HOURS LATER...

Zzz

ding
ding
ding
HELLO?
snort?

HA-HA! SEE, I TOLD YOU MERIDA'D KEEP THINGS RIGHT IN ORDER!
?

DID THEY GET THEIR BATH?
ON IT.
End

BACK TO NATURE

EMBROIDERY

HAIR OF THE GIRL

BATTLE POETRY

MERIDA, WE NEED TO DISCUSS THE CLAN BANQUET.
I KNOW, I'LL WATCH THE TRIPLETS.

I ALSO WANT YOU TO RECITE SOMETHING FOR ENTERTAINMENT. YOU NEED TO PRACTICE YOUR PUBLIC SPEAKING.
OH MUM, WHAT?!

DON'T FUSS, THE BANQUET NEEDS SOME REFINED ENTERTAINMENT. SOMETHING SOOTHING, GENTLE...

CAN I USE-
NO BATTLE-AXES, MERIDA.

MY LORDS, THE PRINCESS MERIDA WILL NOW RECITE FOR YOU.
SIIIIGH

"O MY LUVE'S LIKE A RED, RED ROSE, THAT'S NEWLY SPRUNG IN JUNE:"

"O MY LUVE'S LIKE THE MELODIE, THAT'S SWEETLY PLAY'D IN TUNE."

I'LL WAKE 'EM UP... AHEM
"AND EACH MAN FOUGHT HARD WITH MACE AND LANCE PELL MELL,"

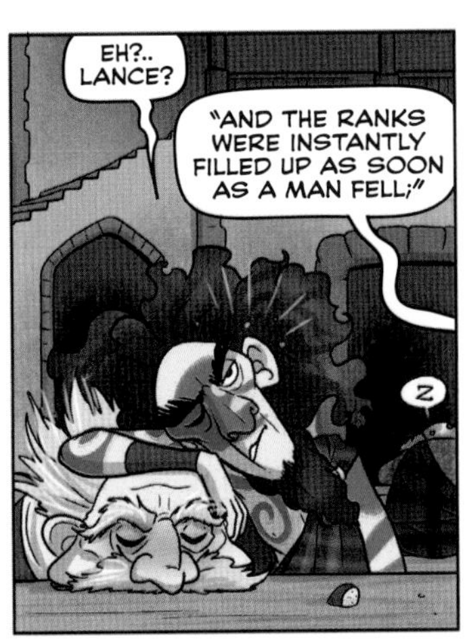

EH?.. LANCE?
"AND THE RANKS WERE INSTANTLY FILLED UP AS SOON AS A MAN FELL;"
Z

"AND THE COUNT BOLDLY CHARGED THE BLACK PRINCE. AND CRIED, YIELD YOU, SIR KNIGHT, OR I'LL MAKE YOU WINCE!"

NOW THAT'S POETRY!
IT IS?

INSOMNIA

FAIR PLAY

MATCHMAKER

SO... YOU WANT TO MEET NEW PEOPLE, BUT YOU'RE... AFRAID?
AYE.

MAYBE IF WE START WITH YOUR APPEARANCE, PROUD MACGUFFIN STOCK...

SAY, A NICE LASSIE SAYS HELLO. WHAT COULD YOU WEAR TO MAKE YOU FEEL CONFIDENT?

OKAY, MIGHT BE OVERDOING IT A WEE STRETCH.
End

ARCHERY FORM

THE MOST IMPORTANT PART OF ARCHERY IS PROPER FORM.
THAT SO?

WHAT D'YE KNOW, BULL'S-EYE!
SEE? FORM.
End

MY FATHER

MY FATHER MAKES ME RECITE THE FAMILY TREE–EVERY NIGHT!

HIS FATHER MAKES HIM PRACTICE PUBLIC SPEAKIN'!
GOOD LUCK WI' THAT...
I'M AFFA FORFAUCHAN!

MY MOTHER MAKES ***ME*** DO EMBROIDERY!
GAWAAAAH!

MY FATHER MAKES ME WASH HIS ***KILTS.***
DINGWALL WINS!
End

HOGMANAY

WAKEY, WAKEY! EGGS 'N' BAKEY! TIME TO MEET AN' GREET A **BRAND NEW YEAR!**

DAAAAD, THAT'S NOT 'TIL **TONIGHT.** LET ME REST FIRST!

BUT IT'S **HOGMANAY!** THE BIGGEST PARTY OF THE **YEAR!** AND WE'RE THROWING IT!
SNIFF

BUT I'M JUST NOT READY TO **CATCH** IT YET...
MAUDIE, FRESH WATER! MAKE IT **COLD.**

"CLEAN THE VESTIGES OF YEAR PAST, MERIDA!" YE JUST WANT ME TO CLEAN THE FIREPLACE, **SAY SO!**

WHAT'S THIS? I TOLD MUM I DIDN'T BORROW THIS! I DON'T EVEN LIKE IT!

WHAT, **ANOTHER** ONE?
TAK

FWOOSH!!
THIS AULD ACQUAINTANCE WILL **NOT** BE FORGOT, I TELL YOU... PFFT

WELL NOW, THE VESTIGES ARE CLEAR, TIME FOR A WEE CLEANSING **FIRE!**

I KNEW IT!

HOLD STILL, YE ROTTEN WEE CHIMNEY SQUIRRELS!

THE POINT OF SWEEPING IS TO GET IT **INTO** THE BUCKET, MERIDA...

End

EYES CLOSED

End

Written by Georgia Ball, Paul Benjamin, Steffie Davis, Caleb Goellner, Geoffrey Golden, Emma Hambly, Oliver Ho, Arie Kaplan, Megan Kearney, Charli McEachran, Deanna McFadden, Amy Mebberson, Christopher Meades, Tea Orsi, Pat Shand, and Patrick Storck.

Illustrated by Amy Mebberson, Egle Bartolini, Dylan Bonner, Chris Dreier, Nicole Dalcin, Jason Flores-Holz, Brianna Garcia, Nolen Lee, Mitch Leeuwe, and Steph Lew.

Colored by Amy Mebberson, Wes Dzioba, Matt Herms, Paul Little, and Donovan Yaciuk.

Series edited by Steffie Davis, Jennifer Hale, and Deanna McFadden.

Lettered by AndWorld Design and Nicole Dalcin.

Special thanks to Eugene Paraszczuk, Julie Dorris, Chris Troise, Manny Mederos, Jean-Paul Orpinas, Deron Bennett, Jesse Post, and Amy Weingartner.

Disney Princess

COVER GALLERY

Princess #1, February 2016, cover by Amy Mebberson

Princess #2, March 2016, cover by Amy Mebberson

Princess #3, May 2016, cover by Amy Mebberson

Princess #4, June 2016, cover by Amy Mebberson

Princess #5, August 2016, cover by Amy Mebberson

Princess #6, September 2016, cover by Amy Mebberson

Princess #7, November 2016, cover by Amy Mebberson

Princess #8, December 2016, cover by Amy Mebberson

Princess #9, February 2017, cover by Amy Mebberson

Princess #10, March 2017, cover by Amy Mebberson

Princess #11, June 2017, cover by Dylan Bonner

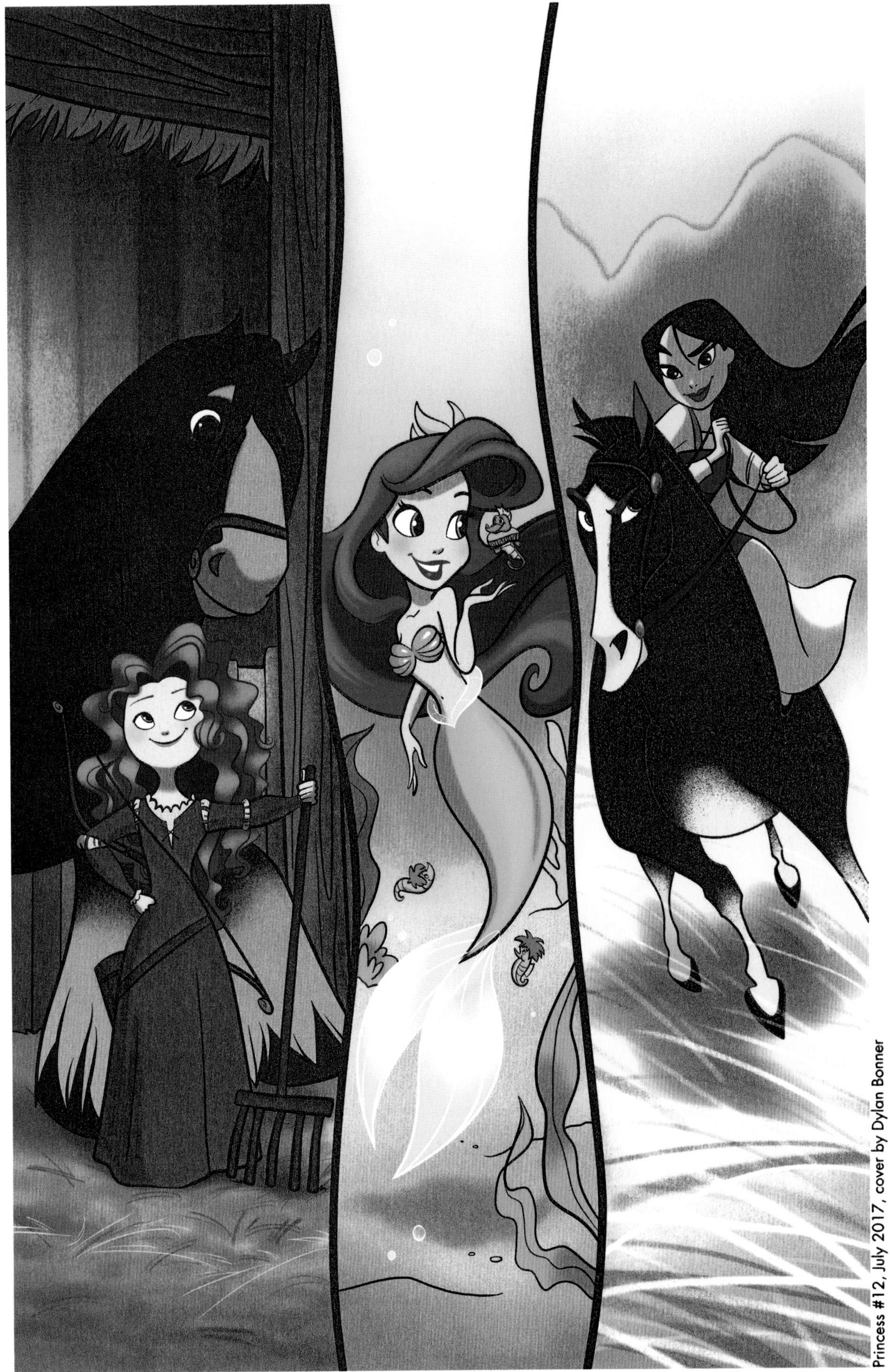

Princess #12, July 2017, cover by Dylan Bonner

Princess #13, September 2017, cover by Dylan Bonner

Princess #14, November 2017, cover by Dylan Bonner